For a second she relived the terror of the cows stampeding around her.

The last time she'd suffered such uncontrollable panic was the day Amy had been taken from her arms. No one had come to rescue her then. But this afternoon, her knight in shining. . .hmm. . .blue jeans. . .had ridden up on his steed to save the day.

She'd never felt anything more heavenly than the strength of Cade's arms scooping her up and making her safe. Heat crept up her face as she remembered how she'd clung to him. He'd worked half a day before the cows got out, but when she'd buried her nose in his shirt, the laundry soap smell that still lingered there had erased the dust from her senses just as his calm, steady voice had eased away her terror.

She trusted him. Other than Julie and her mother, she hadn't trusted another human being since she was seventeen. Warning bells jangled in her head. If Cade refused to help her find Amy, she had to be prepared to move on. She'd avoided entanglements for seven years.

CHRISTINE LYNXWILER and her husband, Kevin, live in the foothills of the beautiful Ozark Mountains of their home state, Arkansas. Christine currently serves as the president of American Christian Romance Writers, an international writing organization with over 250 members. Her favorite thing to do is spend time with her husband and daughters together as a family. She considers the opportunity to share her stories with Barbour's wide audience one of the greatest blessings God has given her. Christine has written two novellas, which are included in Barbour anthologies. *In Search of Love* is her first **Heartsong Presents**.

In Search of Love

Christine Lynxwiler

Heartsong Presents

To Billie and Elva Lynxwiler & Jana and Dan Nichols—for accepting me into your family by marriage and welcoming me into your hearts by choice. The times we've spent working cattle and just having a good time at the "farm" made it possible for me to dream up the "Circle-M" adventures.

Thanks to my crit buds—Tracey Bateman, Susan Warren, Tamela Hancock Murray, Lianne Lopes, Patty Hall, Kathleen Paul, Susan Downs, Sandy Gaskin, Jan Reynolds, and Lynette Sowell!

As always, thanks to Kevin, Kristianna, and Kaleigh, for being the best family a gal could ever wish for. I love you all so much.

And most of all, thanks to my Heavenly Father for blessing me beyond measure and loving me in spite of myself.

A note from the author:
I love to hear from my readers! You may correspond with me by writing:

> **Christine Lynxwiler**
> **Author Relations**
> **PO Box 719**
> **Uhrichsville, OH 44683**

ISBN 1-58660-688-3

IN SEARCH OF LOVE

All Scripture quotations are taken from the King James Version of the Bible.

All of the characters and events in this book are fictitious. Any resemblance to actual persons, living or dead, or to actual events is purely coincidental.

PRINTED IN THE U.S.A.

prologue

Annalisa's hands trembled as she clutched her sister to her chest and buried her face in the baby's silken curls. Drawing courage from the familiar scent, she looked up to confront the social worker. The stiff-backed woman stood, arms extended, waiting. Waiting for Annalisa to do the impossible.

"Miss Miller, I know you think it's for the best, but you can't take Amy from me." Annalisa eyed the sheriff standing behind the woman and struggled to sound grownup, in spite of her rising terror. "I'll be eighteen in less than a year. I can be a good mother to her."

Ignoring her plea, the woman pried the baby from Annalisa's arms. "You know she'll be better off with a mother and father who can give her what she needs." The older woman balanced the baby with one arm and tossed the diaper bag strap across her shoulder. "We've been through this repeatedly. If I could've found you two a foster placement together I would have. Unfortunately, I couldn't."

Miss Miller shifted Amy's weight to the other side of her angular body and peered down her hawk-like nose at Annalisa. Her expression softened slightly and a tendril of hope sprouted in the girl's heart, only to be squashed by the social worker's next words. "Besides, it's time for you to have a life. You took care of your mother after your father left, and you've been more of a mother than a sister to Amy since her birth. That's a heavier load than most grown women have to bear."

Annalisa couldn't hold back the sobs any longer as she

pleaded with the woman who held her beloved Amy in her arms. "You can't take her from me. . ." She discarded any vestige of pride and fell to her knees. Fighting hysteria, she clutched the woman's skirt and squeezed the rough navy polyester as if it were a lifeline. "She's all I have left. I love her."

Miss Miller glanced at the sheriff, who stood motionless across the room. "I've tried to reason with her." She nodded toward Annalisa. "She's all yours. Maybe you can make her understand."

"She has just lost her mother. I can see why—" The older man moved toward Annalisa.

"Your sympathy doesn't change reality," Miss Miller boomed. Baby Amy's face crumpled, and she gave a startled cry.

Annalisa instinctively reached for her again.

"I'm leaving with the baby. You need to be sure the girl gets to the social services office so the Johnsons can pick her up."

The sheriff gave Annalisa another sympathetic look, but nodded.

Miss Miller pulled away from Annalisa's clutching hands. She stepped around her and strode to the door, then turned back. "Take my advice, young lady. The best thing you can do is forget and move on."

Annalisa clambered to her feet, infused with a sudden spurt of inner strength. "I'll never forget." She stared at the crying baby, memorizing every nuance of the precious face. "I'll find you, Amy. I promise, I'll find you!"

one

Annalisa Davis grimaced as her car bounced along the washboard road. The crunch of gravel resounded through the interior, making the already disjointed cell phone conversation more difficult.

"You know, Julie, at first, I thought it was a stroke of luck finding out about this ranch. Now I'm not so sure." She tucked the phone under her chin and waved at a man on a tractor who had pulled over to let her pass. "You should see this road. Mr. McFadden's secretary said it was out in the sticks. Big-time understatement."

"Well, I tried to talk you out of going. What's six more months after waiting seven years? Or you could've used someone else." Julie's voice faded in and out, but Annalisa had heard the speech so many times in the last few weeks she knew it by heart.

"I couldn't wait any longer once I had the money saved." Annalisa slowed the car to a crawl and took her sunglasses off, squinting at a weathered sign. "And, like I told you before, Cade McFadden is the best."

"I know—"

Before her friend could launch into her ongoing campaign against this trip, Annalisa broke in, excitement edging her voice. "Jules, this is it. The sign says Circle-M Ranch. I actually found it. Gotta go now. I'll call you tonight."

"Okay. . .good luck."

"It'll take more than luck. You'd better be praying for

me like you promised."

Armed with Julie's assurance of continued prayer, Annalisa said a hurried good-bye. She flipped the little phone shut, then turned her car into the lane. She rolled her window down and eyed the cows munching away in the pastures.

Trying not to dwell on the four-footed inhabitants of the ranch, she concentrated instead on the lush green grass that carpeted the rolling hills as far as she could see. Whipped-cream clouds decorated the blue sky.

The scene reminded Annalisa of a child's drawing. She couldn't remember ever seeing such crisp, vibrant colors in the city.

Lord, please let me find a place like this to raise Amy. But first, help me find her.

Her little car topped a hill, and Annalisa gasped. A massive ranch house stood in the middle of numerous outlying barns and sheds. Several vehicles, all of the four-wheel-drive variety, were scattered around the yard. How many people had she signed on to cook for? Maybe Julie was right . . .maybe she was crazy.

Biting back a wave of panic, she pulled her car in front of the house and parked. What had she been thinking? When she'd struck up a friendship with Mr. McFadden's secretary, and consequently begged her way into this job, it had seemed like such a good plan.

The reality of providing nourishing meals for several large, hungry men sent doubt coursing through her. She was a good cook, but she'd never cooked in huge amounts before.

Bottom line, she reminded herself, squaring her shoulders—she'd do whatever it took to get close to Cade McFadden.

&

Cade hammered the last board into place and turned to grin at his brother. "That ought to do it, Holt. At least for today." After wiping the sweat from his face with his shirtsleeve, he readjusted his Stetson and nodded toward the house. "I'm starving. The cook was supposed to arrive this afternoon. Maybe we'll have food fit to eat tonight."

"Yep. Aunt Gertie tries but, bless her heart, she's not a cook." Holt chuckled.

Cade hung the hammer on a peg above the workbench, then he and Holt started up the hill toward the house.

"Look over there, Cade." Holt pointed at a corral up by the middle barn where two men were hammering furiously. "Dad and Jake were so sure they'd beat us. We proved them wrong, didn't we?"

"Sure did." Cade nodded toward the roof of the neighboring barn where their other brother was wielding a paintbrush. "What do you suppose Clint's excuse will be for not beating us?"

"Well, you know, as a fireman he's not used to carrying anything besides an ax and a high pressure hose when he walks on a roof. That brush and bucket of tar in his hand probably threw him off," Holt retorted with a laugh.

"Hey. Watch it! You don't want us to start making politician jokes, do you?" Cade teased, glad to see his brother's normal good humor returning. Holt was starting to get over the breakup of a long-term relationship. So far, he'd refused to share the details with the family. "Man, I still can't believe you all came up here this weekend. It's like an old-fashioned barn-raisin'." Cade flashed Holt another grin and slapped him on the back. "I don't deserve to have such a family, but I thank God I do."

Cade pulled open the screen door and let his brother go ahead of him into the mudroom. The perfect room for a ranch, it caught all the dirt and grime of a long hard day. A double sink in the corner allowed both brothers to scrub up at the same time.

As Cade walked beside Holt up the rock steps and through the sliding glass doors that led into the main house, he thought again of how God had blessed him. He knew his family's presence was their way of letting him know they were rooting for him. His dream of a ranch for troubled kids was about to become a reality, and he couldn't have done it without them.

Holt slid the door open and a savory aroma rushed to greet them. The men exchanged a wide grin. Cade's stomach rumbled as they hurried inside.

He grabbed his seventy-year-old aunt by the waist and swung her around in a mock square dance.

She giggled and slapped his arm. "Now, Cade, you stop it. I'm too old for that."

Cade froze in mid-swing and looked at his brother. "Holt, do you think Aunt Gertie is too old to do a little dos-si-do?"

"No, she's definitely not too old, but now that you mention it, you look a little out of breath." Holt and Aunt Gertie broke into laughter.

"I walked right into that one, didn't I?" Cade asked, shaking his head. "Time for a subject change." He pointed in the direction of the kitchen. "I see. . .or should I say, smell. . .you got our new cook all settled in. I bet you're glad to have a female to talk to. It'll give you somebody to sit on the porch and visit with at night."

"Yeah," Holt chimed in. "You can compare grandkids."

"Oh, I don't think so." Aunt Gertie pursed her lips, but didn't say anymore.

"I'm starving. What time's supper?" Cade had long since

stopped trying to figure out his aunt. Or any woman, for that matter.

"In about half an hour, I think."

"Holt and I'll get quick showers. Can you send the rest of them to do the same when they give up out there?"

"That won't be long," Holt added with a snort. "They're about to run out of daylight."

❧

As he slipped into a clean pair of faded jeans, Cade wondered for the tenth time if he was in over his head, trying to start a boys' ranch. Day after tomorrow, a vanload of city kids would arrive and he was supposed to whip them into shape. Figuratively, of course.

Using all his influence, and some he'd borrowed from Holt, he had pulled enough strings to get the ranch going on a trial basis. A wry grin tugged at Cade's mouth. Who would have thought having a politician in the family would be a good thing?

The grin faded as he remembered how imperative it was that the ranch succeed. No one in his old circle understood the importance of a place like this. "A guilt offering," his sometimes-girlfriend had called it in her agitation at his six-month leave of absence.

Maybe the project had germinated from his paralyzing guilt. But he'd done months of research and, when he'd realized how few alternatives these kids had, he'd felt ashamed. Ashamed that he'd never thought of helping before.

Years of hard work and relentless determination had moved McFadden Investigations from a tiny rented office on the wrong side of Little Rock to its new location in a restored colonial manor in the Quapaw Quarters.

Being a private investigator had been Cade's fantasy since

he was a boy. For the first few years, his dream career had surpassed his expectations.

Even though he had officially taken a leave of absence, he couldn't stomach the idea of ever going back. He'd done enough damage to last a lifetime.

For the sake of his loyal employees he'd resisted the urge to sell the business. So his office manager, Mrs. Spencer, ran the place with an iron hand, efficiently dividing the caseload between four investigators.

Pain stabbed Cade as he thought of the missing children cases from all over the region that came into his office. Sometimes the price for success was too high.

ᔧ

Annalisa blew a renegade curl away from her sweat-dampened forehead. She peered into the oven at the golden biscuits, then grabbed two pot holders and eased both pans out. Eyeing them critically, she hoped there was enough to go around.

The woman who had helped her get settled in—"Aunt Gertie," she'd insisted Annalisa call her—said there would be five men at supper tonight.

Annalisa raised the lid on the roast and vegetables, inhaling the scent as it filled the room. Aunt Gertie had invited her to sit down with them for dinner, but she'd decided to eat in the kitchen. Looking at the big wall clock, she breathed a sigh of relief as she realized everything was done right on time.

Please, Lord, let there be enough food, she prayed.

The swinging doors burst open, and Aunt Gertie hurried in. "Oh! Everything smells delicious. Let's get this on the table."

The two women carried steaming dishes into the dining room and set them on an oak table that could easily accommodate ten people. Benches lined both sides and high-backed chairs with wicker seats stood at each end. Annalisa quickly brought out glasses filled with ice and set them on the runner that covered the antique buffet in the corner. When the pitchers of tea were in place, she stood back and surveyed her work.

"Annalisa, you've done a beautiful job." Aunt Gertie offered a wry chuckle. "If you could have seen supper last night. . . Everything was either charred beyond recognition or too raw to eat." She put her arm around Annalisa's waist. "I sure am glad you're here."

Startled by the physical display of affection, Annalisa awkwardly patted the tiny woman's hand. "Me too. Smelling all this food is making me ravenous though. I think I'll go eat." She left Aunt Gertie to ring the dinner bell and escaped to the kitchen.

Grabbing the plate she'd prepared for herself beforehand, she sank down on the barstool. After a quiet prayer of thanks, she ate in silent contemplation of her large undertaking.

Loud laughs from the dining room punctuated the silence in the kitchen. The deep voices rattled through the walls, and Annalisa realized how long it had been since she'd been around a man's voice on a regular basis. Really not since her dad left. Julie's father had died two years before she and her mother had welcomed Annalisa into their home.

She swallowed her last bite of food and leaned the barstool back, balancing it on two legs. Securing herself with her feet under the bar, she reached up with both hands to lift her heavy curls off her neck.

A deep, masculine voice sounded nearby. "Now, Aunt Gertie, I want to thank the cook. As good as that supper was, I might just have to do like that plaque on the wall says and 'Kiss the Cook.'"

Her tired brain didn't process the words from the dining room fast enough. At the sound of the swinging doors opening behind her, Annalisa lost her balance and the barstool tipped over backward, landing with a thump. Still seated in the stool, which was now flat on its back, she lifted her gaze and offered a weak smile to the bewildered man staring down at her.

His smoky blue eyes widened. The small hint of a smile around his chiseled lips told her an all-out grin from this man might be more than she could stand. She couldn't help but wonder if he'd really meant it when he said he wanted to kiss the cook.

two

Cade stared at the startled woman on his kitchen floor. The riotous brown curls splaying out from her head seemed to go on for miles. Her eyes were the color of melted chocolate. Gold flecks sparkled in them now, reminding him of buried treasure, and mesmerizing him into silence.

Beneath the embarrassment in her gaze, he saw a strong emotion he couldn't quite identify. Longing, maybe, or desperation. Suddenly, it seemed more likely her eyes were hiding secrets rather than treasure.

"Cade, now look what you've done." Before Cade could move, Aunt Gertie bustled over to the girl and reached to help her. "Honey, are you okay?"

The brunette nodded and scrambled to her feet, quickly righting the barstool and putting it in its proper place. Cade noticed she stood only a few inches shorter than his six-feet-two height.

Red-faced, she met his gaze and, unlike so many tall girls he'd known, she held her shoulders back and her head up. "I'm fine," she said, extending a long, slender hand. "I'm so sorry. What a klutz I am. You must be Mr. McFadden. I'm Annalisa Davis, your new cook. I know it sounds like a double name, but it's just one word. . .Annalisa." She shrugged. "Don't worry if you mangle it. You'll probably get the hang of it eventually. Most people do." With a self-deprecating smile, she added, "Unless I'm fired on the grounds of incredible clumsiness, in which case you can replace me with someone

named Jane or Sue, and you won't have to worry about it."
Again her gaze connected with his and held.

Cade took her hand, astonished at the unexpected presence
of this beautiful, albeit babbling, young woman and found
himself rushing to reassure her. "Fired? Don't be ridiculous.
The accident was my fault. I shouldn't have barged in on you."

Annalisa's face flushed a deeper crimson as she smoothly
removed her hand from his. "Thanks for being such a good
sport," she said with a sheepish grin.

"No problem."

Annalisa nodded toward the dining room. "If y'all are done
in there, I'll just quietly do the dishes." Her lips twitched. "I
promise not to break anything."

He chuckled. Secrets or not, a lady who could laugh at
herself was rare. "Call me Cade. And you're not getting
away before I do what I came in here to do." Cade realized
by the deer-in-the-headlights look on Annalisa's face that she
had heard his silly comment about kissing the cook. "That is,
to thank you for such a wonderful meal. We enjoyed it
tremendously."

He saw her shoulders relax, and he bit back a smile at her
obvious relief as she turned to tackle the pots and pans.
Wouldn't his brothers kid him if they knew how happy a
beautiful woman seemed to be to avoid a kiss from him?

Then he spotted his three brothers and his father peering in
through the wide doorway, grinning broadly. Shooting them a
dirty look, he reached over and closed the double doors, not
caring that it barely missed Jake's nose.

He turned back to the women, ignoring Aunt Gertie's slight
smile. "Annalisa, if there's anything I can do to help you settle in, or if you have any questions, just let me know."

"Yes, Sir. I will." Annalisa paused in the middle of wiping

the counter, as if waiting for him to leave.

He crossed the room and dropped a kiss on his aunt's cheek. " 'Night, Aunt Gertie. Annalisa, thanks again for supper."

He slipped out of the kitchen and padded down the hallway, thinking about his mysterious new cook. In the den, he found the men sitting around, long legs sprawled out, pretending to be engrossed in an old western on television. They ignored him for a minute, until Holt looked up with a twinkle in his eyes and drawled, "What happened to the famous McFadden charm, Bro? You must be getting old."

His brothers snickered.

"Wait a minute," Jeb said, holding up his hands. "I'm old, and I've still got it." He regarded his oldest son and shook his head in mock dismay. "It must have skipped a generation."

Cade couldn't keep from joining in as his brothers roared with laughter.

&

After setting the alarm, Annalisa changed into her long flannel gown, then reached up and unfastened the locket from around her neck. As she had each night for the past seven years, she opened it and stared at the two pictures—a teenage girl and a chubby-cheeked baby. Curling her fingers around the treasure, she pressed it tightly against her face. With a deep sigh, she clicked it shut and placed it carefully on the nightstand beside the small lamp.

After she said her prayers, she burrowed under the covers and lay staring at the shadows on the ceiling, wishing she could live the last few moments over. She'd worked hard for this opportunity, and sheer determination had kept her from falling apart after her little fiasco. But even determination hadn't stopped her from babbling, a habit she had when she was nervous. Cade McFadden probably thought he'd hired a lunatic.

≈

Cade stretched farther over the edge of the cliff to see where the sound was coming from. About a foot down the side, a small boy grasped a tiny branch, his feet dangling above the seemingly bottomless canyon below. As the branch bent, the boy's whimpers grew louder. Just as the twig broke, Cade lunged and grunted with relief when their hands connected.

His relief melted into horror as the child's hand became slick, as if covered in oil. In spite of Cade's desperate attempt to hold on, the little hand slid from his grip. He screamed and leaped forward over the precipice, grabbing with both arms.

With a jolt, Cade connected with something solid. The floor. Relief coursed through him. He'd been dreaming again. Cold sweat trickled under his T-shirt. Shaking, he eased himself up onto the bed, gave the pillow a punch, and squinted at the clock. 2:04.

He got up and made his way into the master bathroom. Pulling a little cup from the holder on the wall, he caught a glimpse of himself in the vanity mirror. In the dim light, he looked like a crazed man. His dark hair stood on end, and a sheen of perspiration glistened on his face. Tonight's dream, just like all the rest, had been so real.

These terrible nightmares—each one involving a child in danger—had plagued him in the city. Since he'd come to the ranch two weeks ago, he'd slept like a baby. It had seemed that God had granted him the peace he'd asked for. Until tonight.

As he filled the cup with water and drank the cold liquid down, he realized why the dreams had resurfaced. Annalisa Davis represented a threat to his newfound peace. Her face haunted him, something he'd seen in her eyes. . .a deep need. She wasn't just a cook, he was sure of that. So why was she here?

Was her reason for coming to the Circle-M personal, or did it have something to do with his last case? She could be a reporter. She had the confidence for it, he thought, remembering her smooth recovery from the accident in the kitchen.

Frustration and anger built up in his chest. Sleep had never seemed further away. Even if she was with the media, which he had to admit was doubtful after all this time, that still didn't explain the look in her eyes. Job, or no job, she had personal reasons for coming up here.

He slowly walked back to the bed and climbed in. He had to get some sleep. Closing his eyes again, he could see her, shoulders back, chin lifted high, as though she had something to prove. Couldn't anything be simple? A beautiful woman landed at his feet—with hair like an angel and eyes he could drown in—and his private investigator mind couldn't help but question it.

Lord, please set me free. If it's Your will, Father, help me to forget the past and concentrate on the boys who are coming here Monday for a new start. Create in each of them a clean heart and an open mind, so I can teach them about You by the way I live. Help me to be the example You want me to be. In Jesus' name, amen.

Drifting off to sleep, Cade thought again of the secrets lurking in his new cook's eyes. *And Lord, please give Annalisa the peace she seeks.*

❧

The next morning, Cade walked down the hall toward the dining room, wishing the bright sunshine had avoided his window instead of sneaking in and prodding his eyelids to open. Each new reason he'd conjured up to explain Annalisa's presence grew worse than the one before. By the time his alarm had gone off, he'd imagined she was a hit man. . .make that hit woman, hired to bump him off.

In no hurry to face the cause of his nocturnal unrest, or anyone else, he slipped out of the house and retrieved the morning paper from the end of the driveway before continuing on to breakfast. Sliding into a vacant chair at the dining room table, he quickly hid behind the front page.

"Cade, if your mother were here, she'd have your hide for reading the paper at the breakfast table."

Surprised by the reprimand, Cade lowered his paper.

His father's big smile belied his gruff voice. "But since she stayed home this weekend, pass me the sports."

With a chuckle, Cade complied, then offered the rest of the paper to his brothers.

Aunt Gertie hurried through the swinging door with a pot of steaming coffee in her hand. Cade watched over the top of the paper as she stopped and opened her mouth in mock dismay at the sight of the male members of the family—each with his nose buried in a section of newspaper.

"Well, can you believe it?" She yanked the comics from Clint's hand and poured coffee in his mug. "I've never seen the likes of such bad manners," she said, as she calmly snatched the business section from Holt and deposited it on the antique buffet. Lips twitching with a suppressed smile, she placed her hands on her hips. "The rest of you gonna give yours up peaceful-like, or am I gonna have to wrestle them from you?"

The men guffawed, but they handed their papers to the tiny woman and were rewarded with a cup of coffee.

"Annalisa worked hard fixing breakfast, and if you know what's good for you, you'll eat it."

"You must've eaten your Wheaties, Aunt Gertie," Jake said with a smile.

"I don't want her to get her feelings hurt, that's all." Gertie patted Jake on the shoulder and moved on to the swinging doors.

"Oh, no," Clint muttered. "Breakfast must be awful if Aunt Gert thinks we'll hurt the cook's feelings over it."

Cade groaned. He'd known she wasn't a cook, and now she was about to prove it. Last night's meal must have been a fluke.

The swinging doors opened, and Aunt Gertie and Annalisa entered, each holding a rectangular glass dish. Could it possibly be. . . ? Oh, no, it was. . .a casserole. The one thing his dad had sworn he'd never eat. No wonder Aunt Gertie had warned them.

"If I want all my food mashed up together, I'll do it on my plate," Jeb McFadden always said. It was a creed Cade and his brothers had grown up with.

After Annalisa set her dish down on the table and returned to the kitchen, the men's gazes, as if synchronized, swung from the food to Aunt Gertie's stern face. Slowly, they filled their plates, and Cade watched in amazement as all of them, even his dad, took a bite, then smiled. His aunt had her bluff in. But not on him. This was his house, and he wasn't going to tiptoe around an employee's feelings.

Looking down at his plate, he decided rearranging the food a little to make it look like he'd eaten wouldn't hurt anything. Just as he was pushing it around with his fork, he caught Aunt Gertie's watchful eye on him and shoved a bite in his mouth. Bacon, eggs, and cheese had never tasted so good. Making up for lost time, he quickly cleaned his plate.

❧

Annalisa pulled into the church parking lot with minutes to spare. She'd noticed the tiny building as she drove past yesterday and had hoped to be able to attend worship there today. Sitting in her car, she thanked God there had been no conversations with her boss this morning.

Gertie had helped her with the breakfast dishes, then Annalisa had hurried to her room, dressed for church, and slipped out the door to her car. She'd prepared much of today's lunch ahead of time, so she could be free this morning. If she didn't linger, everything should be fine.

She got out of her car and, after taking a moment to absorb the beauty of God's creation, she strolled into the building. She returned the smiles and nods of the members and found a seat near the back.

The congregation was still talking in subdued tones, waiting for worship to start, when a shadow fell across Annalisa. Startled, she looked up into the blue eyes of Cade McFadden.

"Fancy meetin' you here," he said with a grin.

"You too." Annalisa mustered up an answering smile. She needed to stop feeling so stressed around him. After all, her goal was to convince him to help her. In order to do that, she'd have to get to know him better. "Is the rest of your family with you?"

Cade nodded toward a pew behind her, and Annalisa turned in her seat to see Mr. McFadden, his other three sons, and Aunt Gertie crowded onto a bench two rows back.

"Didn't they save you a seat?" What an inane thing to say. She had just forced herself into inviting him to sit with her.

Sure enough, when he shook his head, she was compelled to ask, "Would you like to sit here? There's plenty of room."

He slid into the empty space beside her just as the service began. Self-conscious, she found it difficult to concentrate on the lesson. *Lord, give me the strength to ignore this man, at least until the service is over.*

❧

Annalisa carefully folded a paper towel and placed it on a

plate. The potatoes were mashed. The rolls were in the oven. The gravy was done. She sighed with relief as she took up the golden brown pieces of chicken. She'd pulled it off. Surely if she could cook for five grown men, the three boys arriving tomorrow should be easy. Of course, only four of those men were going home this afternoon.

Cade McFadden—the reason she had come to this little cattle ranch in northern Arkansas—was staying. Then she'd be left with the one man who seemed to have the power to make her forget why she'd hired on for this job. Her plan to get to know him slowly and gain his trust before asking for his help disappeared when he looked at her with those deep blue eyes.

When she was in his presence, she found her words rushing out in an unchecked stream. So far, she'd been able to keep from blurting out her real reason for being here, but she wondered how strong she'd be when the others were gone.

The doors behind her swished, and she turned, three-pronged fork still in her hand, to face the man who occupied her thoughts.

"You're a good cook. But something makes me think there's more to this story. So, do you mind telling me what you're doing here?"

three

Annalisa prayed for a light tone. "It was the casserole that gave me away, wasn't it?"

Cade's eyes narrowed. "Is cooking what you've done for a living before this? And don't consider lying. I can check it out with one phone call."

"Why would I lie? Can't a girl switch careers without you making a criminal case out of it?" Annalisa's smile felt a little stiff, but she was careful to keep it in place. "If my work is unsatisfactory, Mr. McFadden, then I insist you tell me."

She watched her boss run his hand through his hair in exasperation. He'd just opened his mouth to respond when Aunt Gertie bustled in.

"Annalisa, you are truly a wonder. I don't know how you changed from your dress so quickly," she said, reaching in to retrieve the pitchers of iced tea from the refrigerator. If she was aware of the tension between boss and employee, she gave no indication. "Why, you've almost got lunch ready. Bless your heart."

"Funny," Cade said in a flat tone Annalisa recognized as slightly sarcastic. "I thought that's what we were paying her for." He turned and walked out of the room.

With shaking hands, Annalisa helped carry the dishes to the table, using Aunt Gertie as a shield between herself and Cade. She sensed his gaze boring into her, but refused to look his way.

Back in the kitchen, she tackled the dishes immediately,

ignoring the plate of food she'd prepared for herself. The close call with Cade had annihilated her appetite.

It was only a matter of time now. If she didn't divulge her secret, he would ferret it out. His private investigator background wouldn't allow anything less. Maybe tonight when his family left, she should sit down and be straight with him. Surely he wouldn't toss her out on her ear in the dark, especially considering this was the middle of nowhere. Still, remembering how his eyes had burned when he questioned her, she wasn't so sure.

A month ago she'd called Cade's Little Rock office, only to be told Mr. McFadden wasn't taking any new cases at that time. Hoping to change his mind, she'd gone there in person. Mrs. Spencer had been sympathetic, and she and Annalisa had gotten along well. She finally told Annalisa the truth—Cade had taken a six-month leave of absence to start a ranch for troubled boys.

While they were talking, the phone rang and, though she studied the pictures on the wall, Annalisa couldn't help but overhear the secretary's end of the conversation. Her boss wanted her to hire a cook for the ranch. After chatting with Mrs. Spencer for awhile, Annalisa had gathered her nerve and commented on the job opening.

Offering references, she explained she had recently taken her own leave of absence from her position as bookkeeper for a prestigious catering firm in Atlanta. After years of the hustle and bustle, the idea of simple ranch life was very appealing, she'd continued. Even though it wasn't her profession, she was a good cook, she'd assured the woman, and she might be willing to make the sabbatical permanent.

Mrs. Spencer got another phone call, and Annalisa had taken advantage of the opportunity to excuse herself from the room. In the hallway, she'd used her cell phone and called her boss in Atlanta. His wife had been filling in for her while she was gone, and apparently the woman was enjoying the change of pace.

They had no problem extending Annalisa's unpaid vacation. She'd brought up the cook position and ignored her boss's good-natured jibes about the possibility of him applying for a bookkeeping job. Since he was a Christian, he reminded her teasingly, he could only say she was an excellent employee. He couldn't vouch for her cooking, but he did agree to be a reference.

Annalisa hurried back in to tell the office manager she'd be happy to relocate to the small ranch just south of the Arkansas/Missouri border. Thrilled to find a ready-made applicant, the woman had checked Annalisa's references and hired her on the spot.

Any guilt was laid to rest as she left the office when Mrs. Spencer winked and said, "If you happen to find a chance to mention your problem to Mr. McFadden, that's between you and him. I, personally, believe it would do him good to keep his finger in PI work. As a matter of fact, I think you might be just what he needs."

Annalisa squeezed the water from the dishrag. Would Cade McFadden agree with his trusted secretary? She suspected not. Wiping off the counter, she smiled as Aunt Gertie came in carrying an armload of plates.

She rushed to take the burden from the older woman. "You don't have to do that. I can clear the table."

Gertie pointed to Annalisa's plate and shook her head. "Child, you haven't even eaten yet. Sit down and eat, and I'll put these plates in the dishwasher."

Annalisa's protests were overridden by the small, but

forceful, woman, and she found herself seated at the bar, eating, while Aunt Gertie loaded the dishwasher. When the doors swished again, she cringed. Great. Just what she needed—for Cade to think she was shirking her duties.

Not looking back, she watched Aunt Gertie's face light up. "Cade, Sweetie, I bet you came in to thank Annalisa for the wonderful lunch. She scrubbed pots and pans while we ate, and I insisted she sit down and eat now."

"No, actually I came in to let you know Dad and the guys are leaving. And to tell you that you two will be on your own until late tonight." He crossed into Annalisa's line of vision, but this time it was he who kept his head turned away from her. He hugged his aunt lightly. "I'm going to head to Little Rock and pick up some things from my house that I wanted to have here when the boys come tomorrow. Think you can hold down the fort until I get back? I'll probably be late."

Aunt Gertie wiped her hands on the faded dishtowel looped through the drawer handle. "I'll go out and tell them bye. We girls will make it just fine by ourselves, won't we, Annalisa?"

Annalisa nodded and sighed with relief when she heard the kitchen door close behind her. Pushing her plate away, she propped her elbows on the bar and buried her face in her hands.

"We'll discuss it when I get back." Her heart jumped in her throat when she heard a deep voice at her ear.

Turning around, she met Cade's glare with a silent nod. He turned on his heel and strode from the room.

⋅⋅⋅

When Cade eased his four-wheel-drive wagon off the highway, he had a disconcerting realization. His afternoon and evening had been spent trying to erase the image of Annalisa when he'd left. Her face had gone pale at the sight of him, and her eyes had grown wide. She had nodded with dignity at his hard words, and Cade had to restrain himself from going back and telling her to forget it—he didn't care what she was hiding.

He was unfamiliar with the protective instincts Annalisa had awakened. He'd always been too busy with work to pursue a woman, instead drifting in and out of a casual relationship with a friend's sister, a woman who needed protecting about as much as a barracuda. She'd started going to church with him, and he'd thought they might have a future. He'd even prayed about it. But when Cade had first decided to open the boys' ranch, she'd made it clear she wasn't interested in ranch life, no matter how temporary.

She had broken up with him, then quickly married a prominent Little Rock businessman, satisfying her apparent desire to belong to the country club set. Cade's pride had suffered a blow, but he was surprised to realize probing the old wound didn't hurt anymore. He could actually thank God for that unanswered prayer.

When he married, if he ever did, it would be to someone he could trust. . .a woman who shared his faith and understood his values. He'd watched his dad and mom and how their relationship had deepened every year. They were best friends, but that spark between them was still evident. That's what he wanted.

He parked his wagon beside Annalisa's car and thought again of what he would say to her. Tomorrow would be soon enough to decide. The house was dark and still as he approached. Walking quietly down the hall to his bedroom, he saw a muted light under Annalisa's door as if her lamp was still on. He might as well let her know he was home.

He raised his hand to knock and paused in mid-air at the

sound of Annalisa's voice coming from the room. "Julie, I have to convince him. I'll do whatever it takes to find Amy." Cade remained at the door long enough to ascertain she was having a phone conversation, then he moved on to his room. He collapsed into the overstuffed armchair by the window.

A missing person.

Considering she had sought him out, it was probably a child. Of course. . .he had seen it in her eyes but hadn't wanted to acknowledge the pain. He decided to take a different approach and not confront her tomorrow like he had planned. First he would find out details and, when she decided to tell him, he'd be forearmed. In the meantime, he was going to get to know her better. Maybe she'd decide to trust him with the truth.

Was it a lost custody case? Or one where the father took the child even though Annalisa had custody? If it had been a straightforward kidnapping, she surely would have blurted it out as soon as she'd met him. His thoughts swirled.

Could she really be a mother? Had she been married? Was she still? Whatever her situation, she obviously had come to him hoping for help. Letting her down easy was the best he could do. But until she asked, he intended to treat her as part of the family here at the Circle-M.

He slowly took his shoes and socks off and stretched out on the bed. His night of poor sleep had caught up with him, and he dozed off fully clothed.

❧

"Good morning, ladies." Cade's cheerful voice rang out as he walked into the kitchen where Annalisa prepared buttered toast and Aunt Gertie poured glasses of milk.

Annalisa cringed and then took a second look at the smiling cowboy. Had Cade received a brain transplant in Little Rock?

Could this be the same man who had issued the ominous promise—"We'll discuss it when I get back"—before leaving yesterday?

"Good morning, Cade," Aunt Gertie said, smiling.

"Good morning, Mr. McFadden," Annalisa echoed.

"I told you. . .call me Cade. After today we're just going to be one big happy family around here. One very big happy family." He chuckled.

Relaxing a little, Annalisa carefully spread butter on the bread. "What time are the boys arriving?"

"Around two-thirty or three," he said. "George Winemiller and his wife Marta are the houseparents, and they've agreed to bring the boys as they come. They will already have eaten." Smiling at Annalisa, he added, "Sandwiches would be fine with me for lunch. How about you, Aunt Gert?"

"That sounds lovely. I'll fix them, Annalisa. That way you can be free until supper—to prepare for the onslaught of boys."

"Oh, Aunt Gertie, you don't have to do that," Annalisa began and then faltered at the woman's quelling look, "uh, I mean, thanks. That would be great."

"Aunt Gertie's training you, I see. It doesn't take long to recognize the iron hand beneath the kid gloves, does it?" Cade aimed a playful grin at Annalisa that took her breath away.

Yeah, a flash of dimples and you melt. You're asking for trouble. Julie had always teased her about her shyness with men, but her best friend never understood the lesson Annalisa had learned early. Men had the power to destroy women. Her mother had been proof of that. Cade and Gertie's mock scuffling brought her back to the present.

"Oh, you." The older woman swatted the dishtowel playfully at her nephew.

Cade wrapped his aunt in a bear hug. "Okay, I admit it. Iron hand or not, I don't know what I'd have done if she hadn't agreed to help me out here."

"I can see that. You're very blessed to have her." Annalisa looked warmly at the woman who had been so kind to her since her arrival yesterday.

"I'm going to take this to go, if you two don't mind." After Cade poured his milk into a plastic cup, he filled his empty glass with water and set it in the sink.

"You work too hard, Cade." Aunt Gertie deftly dumped the water out and placed the glass in the dishwasher.

"Yeah, well, I've got some jobs to finish up before the boys arrive." Grabbing his hat off the counter, he nodded at them. "See y'all later."

After he'd gone, Annalisa turned to Aunt Gertie. "He seemed to be in a better mood today, didn't he?"

"He's under a lot of strain right now, Sweetie. Our Cade is usually as good-natured as they come. But, yes, now that you mention it. . .he did seem more like his old self today, praise God."

Annalisa wanted to question the woman, but hesitated to impose on their budding friendship and decided against it. "Will it hurt your feelings if I follow Cade's example and take my breakfast with me, as well?" She watched the woman, reading her face.

"Not at all, Hon." She put her arm around Annalisa's waist in the way that seemed to come so easily in her family. If she noticed Annalisa stiffening, she was too polite to mention it. "You go on and make the most of your free time."

"I'm going to take a book and go for a walk. I have a new Christian romance I'm right in the middle of reading." She slipped her arm around Aunt Gertie's waist and squeezed. "Besides, I've heard boys want to eat all the time, so I may not have a minute to myself after this morning," Annalisa said with a rueful grin.

After telling Aunt Gertie good-bye, Annalisa grabbed her book from her room. When she slipped out the back door, she could hear hammering coming from the barn on the upper part of the property. Skirting it, in case Cade's sweetness and light act this morning had been for Aunt Gertie's benefit, she walked out toward the back of the lot.

The lot actually held two barns, a corral, and the bunk-house, separated from the house by a split-rail fence. There were two gates coming off the gravel road—one leading out to the barns and the other to the house. They were tied open, and Annalisa had a feeling they were seldom closed.

She paused and raised her face to the sky, soaking in the beauty of the spring day. *Thank you, Lord, for this chance.*

Studying the rolling hills, she spotted one not far away with beautiful shade trees in a ridge along it—a perfect spot to curl up with a book.

She struggled to open the big red gate that barred her way. By the time she reached the hill, she was a little out of breath. Collapsing on the ground under a big oak, she reached in her jeans pocket for a scrunchie and pulled her thick hair up in a ponytail.

She gazed in delight at the pond in the valley that had been hidden from her view until now. The sunlight danced across the water, turning tiny ripples to platinum. She laid her head back and closed her eyes as the warm breeze caressed her face. The tension from the last few days slowly left her. Her heart feeling much lighter, she flipped the book open to her place and allowed herself to become immersed in the words of her favorite author.

When she finished the last page, she looked at her watch

and jumped up with a start. It was past noon. She wanted to get a shower before the kids arrived. Jogging a little, she covered the distance fairly fast, but when she topped the last tiny knoll she stopped short at the scene in front of her. Cows, millions of them from the looks of things, were grazing at the red gate she had left open. A few were already through it.

Horrified, Annalisa fought back tears.

Give me courage, Lord. Please let Cade be nearby.

Taking a deep breath, she ran toward the enormous cows, knowing she had to find Cade and get help before the herd reached the next gate that opened onto the gravel road. A white cow jerked with surprise as she neared it. She screamed, and the cow shot towards the gate. The herd followed, and soon cattle were streaming out into the barn lot. Annalisa dodged a pair of deadly-looking horns and screamed for the only person who could save her—"Cade!"

❧

"Cade!" The panic in the woman's voice sent a shard of fear into Cade's chest. He spun from his path toward the house. Spurred on by the sheer terror in the continued calls of his name, he quickly untied Duke from the fence and jumped up on the startled horse.

Relief coursed through him when he saw Annalisa standing at the back of the herd of cows who thundered out into the barn lot. Maneuvering Duke around, he cut the animals off just as they reached the road gate. Knowing Annalisa might not be able to hear him above the noise of pounding hooves, he vigorously motioned for her to move over.

After he repeated the motion, she ran to the fence and scrambled up the wood railings. Her presence there would make it difficult to herd the cows back into the pasture, but it was a great improvement over standing, frozen, in the middle of the entrance.

When the last cow trotted through, he jumped down and closed the gate. His hat had fallen, and when he walked back to retrieve it, soft sobs reached his ears. Startled, he watched Annalisa, white-faced and trembling, clamber down off the fence. Fighting the urge to enfold her in his arms, he gave her a questioning look. "Annalisa?"

"I'm so sorry. I'll go gather my things. I'm sorry." Her teeth were chattering, and he realized she was in shock.

Forget about propriety. He swooped her up in his arms and tucked her to his chest like a child. A soft flowery scent wafted up to meet him. The trembling in his gut reminded him she definitely wasn't a child.

At her weak protest, he shook his head. "Annalisa," he said in his most calming voice, "everything is okay. No harm done. We're going to go up to the house, and Aunt Gertie will take care of you."

Annalisa offered a heart-wrenching sob and buried her head in his shoulder. She clung to him, clutching his shirt and holding on as if she'd never let go. Cade was touched by her unconditional trust. *Please, God, let me be worthy of this faith she has in me.*

After the way he'd acted yesterday, he was surprised she hadn't kicked and screamed when he picked her up. When she said something he had to lower his head to her mouth to make out the words.

"I knew you'd come. I prayed you would."

Before he could respond, Aunt Gertie came hurrying out of the house. "Oh, Cade! I looked out the window and saw you coming. What happened?" She held the door open as she spoke.

"We had a little run-in with the cows." Cade walked through the kitchen and down the hall to Annalisa's room with his aunt right on his heels.

"Is she hurt?"

"No," Cade said, not wanting to say anything that would embarrass Annalisa. He deposited her on her bed, then turned to face his worried aunt. "A long soak in the tub, and possibly a nap, and I think she'll be as good as new."

Annalisa's soft vulnerability was hazardous to his mental well being. He had to get out of there. "I'm going to grab a sandwich and a shower. Call me if you need me."

"Cade?" Annalisa's voice was barely a whisper.

"Yes?" He turned back, his gaze taking in her pale complexion and frightened eyes.

"Thank you. I can't believe I did that." She put her hands over her face.

"It was my fault."

She peeked out from her hands and shook her head.

"It's true. I forgot to tell you the number one rule on a ranch—always leave a gate exactly like you find it. So if it's closed when you get to it, make sure you shut it behind you, and if it's open when you reach it, leave it open."

She nodded, blushing. Relieved to see some color in her face, he slipped from the room with a nod to his aunt, his pounding heart threatening to betray him with every step.

❧

Annalisa lay on top of the quilted comforter. The bath had revived her some, but Cade's earlier suggestion of a nap sounded inviting. She needed to get her strength up before she faced him again. She'd never been so humiliated in her whole life as she had been in the last couple of days. From the minute she'd literally fallen at his feet the first day, she'd been doing stupid things. But the episode this afternoon had surpassed them all.

For a second she relived the terror of the cows stampeding around her. The last time she'd suffered such uncontrollable panic was the day Amy had been taken from her arms. No one had come to rescue her then. But this afternoon, her knight in shining. . .hmm. . .blue jeans. . .had ridden up on his steed to save the day.

She'd never felt anything more heavenly than the strength of Cade's arms scooping her up and making her safe. Heat crept up her face as she remembered how she'd clung to him. He'd worked half a day before the cows got out, but when she'd buried her nose in his shirt, the laundry soap smell that still lingered there had erased the dust from her senses just as his calm, steady voice had eased away her terror.

She trusted him. Other than Julie and her mother, she hadn't trusted another human being since she was seventeen. Warning bells jangled in her head. If Cade refused to help her find Amy, she had to be prepared to move on. She'd avoided entanglements for seven years.

Blood is thicker than water. Her father had always told her that. She'd wondered for years if he really knew what it meant. Especially after he'd deserted them when he found out her mom was pregnant with Amy. Still she knew it was true.

And so had her mother. The night before she died, she'd called to Annalisa to come talk to her. "Honey, I'm not going to make it much longer." Her once beautiful face was ravaged by the constant pain, and her hair hung dull and lifeless around her rounded shoulders.

"Yes, you are, Mama. You're going to be better soon."

Her mother had shaken her head at Annalisa's forced optimism. She grabbed her daughter's hand in her own. "Listen."

Annalisa hadn't wanted to hear what her mother had to say, and she hoped Amy would wake up and cry. But the old house lay silent, making her mother's whisper ring out in the shabby room. "Don't let them take Amy, Honey. Nobody else will look out for her like you will. Remember, blood is thicker than water."

"I know, Mama. I know." Annalisa nodded, but apparently it hadn't satisfied the dying woman.

"You've always been stronger than me. I'm counting on you now. It's up to you to see to it that the baby has a happy home to grow up in." She brushed Annalisa's hair back and caressed her face with a cold, bony hand. "Promise Mama, okay?"

"I promise."

"Love is the most important thing—"

This time Amy's cries had saved Annalisa from having to make any more promises. But she'd already made the one that counted. To take care of Amy.

The musty smell of long illness faded away, and Annalisa shuddered. How close she'd come to forgetting that promise. In some ways she was no stronger than her mama. No matter whether he used his temper or his charm, her father had always been able to talk Annalisa's mother into things—like leaving their daughter home by herself.

"Josie, she's nine years old," her father would say, as if any nine-year-old could be left for hours at night alone. She remembered one night her parents had gone to a party. Someone had tried to break in the little ramshackle house while she was there by herself. She'd scared them off, then sat by the door holding her daddy's shotgun on her lap until her mom and dad had come in laughing about four in the morning.

Shuddering again, Annalisa willed herself to remember the

faint scent of laundry detergent on Cade's shirt and the security of his strong arms around her as she drifted off to sleep.

≈

Walking down the hall, Annalisa looked down at her khaki pants and white top. Normally, she didn't give a thought to her clothes, but she wanted to make a good first impression on the boys. She was refreshed from her nap, but she knew that after the fiasco today, she couldn't afford any more goof-ups.

"There she is. Are you feeling better, Honey?" Aunt Gertie beamed at her as she entered the living room.

"Yes, much. Thank you." Annalisa decided she'd apologized enough to last a lifetime. Surely a change of subject would be better. She glanced at Cade. "I guess the boys aren't here yet?"

"No, I was just telling Aunt Gert they should be here any minute." Cade's voice radiated excitement. In spite of the embarrassment lingering from their last meeting, Annalisa couldn't keep from smiling at his enthusiasm for his pet project.

"I'm so nervous I can't be still," Aunt Gertie exclaimed. "I'm going to go and make some lemonade."

Annalisa and Cade laughed as the older woman scurried off to the kitchen. "She'll spoil them to death, I'm afraid," Cade said.

Annalisa frowned. "A little spoiling will probably do them a world of good, considering their backgrounds."

"Yes, and Aunt Gertie loves children, regardless of whether they're hers by birth or not."

"I can sympathize with that. I've never given birth, but children have a special place in my heart."

"You've never had a child?" Cade seemed surprised at Annalisa's admission.

"No. I've never been married." Puzzled, she wondered why

he seemed so taken aback.

His scrutinizing gaze so close to hers made the room seem small. Her heart hammered in her chest, but she couldn't imagine what had caused the change in his expression.

When he spoke, it all became horrifyingly clear. "Then, who is Amy?"

four

Several loud, short honks signaled the arrival of Circle-M's newest residents, saving Annalisa from having to answer Cade's blunt question. She breathed a quiet sigh of relief as Cade brushed past her to the front door.

Swinging the wooden door wide open, he waved toward the white van coming up the drive. Annalisa joined him on the front porch, hoping he wouldn't bring up the subject of Amy again. Her fears were alleviated when Aunt Gertie hurried out to meet the new arrivals with them.

Talk about a close call. Annalisa's legs wobbled like spaghetti, and her heart beat so hard she could feel her pulse jumping in her throat. How had he found out about Amy? *Silly,* she scolded herself, *he is a private investigator.*

As she watched the big friendly cowboy greet the Wine-millers and meet each boy with a firm handshake, she shook her head. He seemed so far from a PI right now, but she would do well not to be fooled by the Roy Rogers act.

Aunt Gertie put her arm around Annalisa's waist and propelled her forward. Cade looked up as the women approached and introduced them.

Trying to remember everything Cade had told her about the three boys, Annalisa concentrated her attention on them. Thirteen-year-old Juan scowled at their cheery hellos, but seven-year-old Tim jumped up and down, grabbing Cade's shirt. "Can I ride a horse? Please. I want to ride a horse right now."

The middle boy, who had to be the nine-year-old, stood a little to the side of the others, his gaze cast down. When Cade introduced Matthew, the red-headed boy looked up briefly. Annalisa almost gasped at the pain in his green eyes. He bowed his head again, scuffing the toe of his new boot in the dust with great concentration.

Marta Winemiller smiled at Annalisa and Gertie. "It's good to have not just one woman to talk to, but two." Her blond waist-length hair was straight and fine, with a few streaks of gray. Crow's feet flanked her crystal blue eyes and laugh lines edged her mouth. She had a loveliness that came from a peaceful spirit. Annalisa liked her instantly.

They all made the trek out to the bunkhouse for the newcomers to stash their duffel bags. The boys each staked a claim on a bunk in the great room. George and Marta had a private room in the front corner of the building. A tiny kitchen had been installed, but since Annalisa was doing the cooking for everyone, meals would be served in the main house.

Leaving Gertie and Cade to get them settled in, Annalisa excused herself to begin preparing supper. Safe in the kitchen, she faced the inevitable. The excitement of the boys arriving might buy her a day. . .two at the most. Ready or not, she was going to have to tell Cade about Amy. Would Cade send her packing, or would he be the hero she so desperately needed?

ن

George Winemiller scratched his balding head then ran his hand over the wisps of hair as if trying to stretch them to cover the shiny surface. "I don't know. You handpicked 'em, but they're tough. Winning them over is not going to be easy."

"I never thought this project would be easy, but I think it'll be worth the effort." Cade pushed away the negative words. Getting the boys here had been a huge hurdle, and he'd jumped it. Today he could face anything.

As he and George watched in silence, Tim tentatively reached toward Bubba, one of the more gentle horses. When Tim turned around, the delight on the boy's face won Cade's heart. "His nose is as soft as a pile of mud," Tim yelled.

"He's the one I don't understand, Cade. Why's he here?"

Cade shuddered as he remembered what the social worker had told him when she begged him to add Tim to his bunch of troubled boys. "Nobody wanted him. He has asthma. . .pretty bad, I guess. Even though the doctors say he might outgrow the illness, his folks didn't want to wait. 'Too much trouble,' they said. Then they signed away all claim to him and turned him over to the state."

George cleared his throat. Cade noticed a suspicious moisture in his eyes, and he knew the man was going to do just fine with these boys. He'd been happy to find the Winemillers and was thrilled when they were willing to relocate. Still, a niggling doubt had remained until now.

If only his confidence in his newly hired employees could extend to his kitchen staff. Annalisa intrigued him, but he had serious doubts about her being in it for the long haul. The distressed expression on her face when he'd asked about Amy still lingered in his mind. If she'd be honest with him, he could explain to her why he couldn't ever go back to investigating. Of course, he realized, then she'd probably leave. Maybe it was better not to push her.

He glanced at Juan leaning with his back against the fence, trying to look cool. The sun glinted off his spiked jet-black hair, and a scowl was permanently etched on his handsome face.

Cade nudged George. Old Sweetie, a fifteen-year-old mare, had noticed the boy. The horse ambled up but either the teenager didn't hear her or thought he was too cool to turn around. The horse, apparently dissatisfied with the young man's lack of attention, nuzzled the back of his neck. Juan jumped and yelled in rapid Spanish, wiping frantically at his neck with his hands.

"You speak Spanish?" Cade asked George.

"Not a bit," George said with a grin.

"Me either. Probably a good thing."

"Yep."

The two men stayed where they were when Juan shot past them and into the bunkhouse. Cade glanced over at Matthew and Tim, who were standing nearby. "You boys ever ridden a horse?"

Tim's head jerked up. "No. . ."

"How about you, Matthew?" Cade prodded the other boy, hoping to at least get a view of his face.

After a few seconds of silence, Tim said, "Matthew don't talk."

Cade nodded. That's what the social worker had said. Not that he couldn't. . . He just didn't. "I don't reckon you have to talk to ride a horse. They don't understand much of what you say anyway."

Tim giggled, then wiped the smile away with his grungy hand. "Can I ride the horse? He likes me. Can I, please?"

Cade squatted down to Tim's level and tousled his blond hair. "Tomorrow we'll get you all on horses. But today we're just going to relax and get used to the ranch and each other. Annalisa's fixing us a good supper. What do you say to that, Buddy?"

"All right!" he said, throwing his arms around Cade's neck.

Cade was sure he'd detected interest in the brief glimpse he'd gotten of Matthew's green eyes, but it was gone so quickly, it might have been his imagination. *One day at a time,* he reminded himself. *They didn't get like this overnight, and they're not going to change overnight,* he repeated the social worker's words in his mind.

"George, why don't you go get Juan, and let's take a little walk? I'd like to show y'all the layout of the land, so you can get to know your way around here a little bit." Then Cade turned to the boys. "Wait here and keep Bubba and Old Sweetie company while I run up to the house and tell the women what we're going to do."

He could have sent one of the boys, but to his chagrin, his heartbeat quickened at the thought of another run-in with the cook.

❧

Annalisa watched out the window as Cade came up the back walk to the kitchen door. He gave a cursory knock and then stuck his head in.

"Where's Aunt Gert?" he asked. "And Marta?"

"Your aunt is showing Marta around the house."

"George and I are going to take the boys for a walk. What time will supper be ready?"

"In about half an hour. Is that too soon?"

"No, that'll be fine. See you then."

"Okay, bye." She turned back to the sink as he left, then looked up again, startled, when he poked his head back in.

"Annalisa?"

"Yeah?"

"We have to talk. . .tonight."

Annalisa's heart thudded in her chest, but she knew he was right, so she nodded. "Okay."

What would he say when she told him the truth? Surely he would help her. He had helped so many others. Admittedly, her situation was a little different. Still, she had been wronged, and Amy definitely belonged with her.

Casting her thoughts aside, she finished cutting up the potatoes and carefully lowered them into the hot grease. She'd have to hurry to meet her self-imposed deadline of thirty minutes.

Half an hour later, when the resident males had returned from their walk and washed up, supper was on the table. Cade insisted Annalisa eat at the long table with everyone else. Not wanting to appear ungracious, she sat down with the group.

Cade said grace and then passed each dish around, helping the boys to know what to do. Annalisa noticed how careful he was to set them at ease. His every little action exemplified his concern for them. Surely he would understand about Amy.

"Annalisa, you did a great job on supper. This venison steak is delicious." Cade gave her a warm smile.

"Thanks." She decided his compliment was sincere when the table conversation lulled while everyone enjoyed the food. The ultimate tribute to a good cook, Julie's mom always said— guests who were too busy consuming delicious cooking to talk.

When she stood to clean up, George and Marta exchanged a look.

"Cade, Marta and I thought the boys could take a turn with K.P. What do you think?"

Cade smiled. "That sounds like a fine idea to me, George. Reminds me of summer camp when I was growing up."

Juan rolled his eyes, and Cade motioned to him. "Juan, you and Tim can help tonight. We'll get a chart made out by tomorrow." The boys stood, the younger exuberant and the older reluctant. "Annalisa, would you show Juan how to load the dishwasher?" When she nodded, he added, "Tim, you start carrying the dishes in the kitchen."

Annalisa began to instruct the thirteen-year-old in the fine art of dishwasher loading.

Leaning on the counter, he wiggled his eyebrows and grinned. "What's a pretty chick like you doing in a dump like this?"

Taken aback, but determined to keep her cool, she met his leer with a level gaze. "Cooking for a boys' ranch, last time I checked. Why do you ask?"

Juan blushed, obviously flustered by her calm manner. "Oh. . .no reason." The rest of the lesson was uneventful and there were even a couple of *yes, ma'am*s.

Feeling pretty pleased with herself after everything was cleaned up, Annalisa collapsed on a chair in the den. She rested the back of her head against the soft pillow of the recliner and closed her eyes.

"Tired?"

Annalisa jumped, and her eyes popped open. "Cade! I didn't hear the door open. Are the boys settled in for the night?" Even after a long day, he still managed to look like he'd stepped out of a western magazine ad.

She cast a disgusted glance at her clothes, damp from Juan's first dishwasher lesson, and sat up straighter. Just because she looked like a wrung out mop, didn't mean she had to sit like one.

"Yeah, I went out and made sure they had everything they needed. Aunt Gertie must have been tired too. She turned in early."

"Today's been really exciting," Annalisa offered. *Unfortunately, I'm afraid the excitement is just beginning. He already knows I'm here about Amy, so why am I terrified? If he was going to blow up, he probably would have already.*

"Yes. Now, Annalisa, do you want to tell me why you came here?" Cade's voice was firm, but tinged with understanding.

Annalisa looked down at her hands and tried to find the right words. Unexpected tears filled her eyes. This was the moment she'd been waiting for.

Please, she prayed, *don't let me blow it.*

Cade's soft voice interrupted her silent plea. "Why don't you start by telling me who Amy is?"

Annalisa raised her head and met Cade's gaze. She searched his eyes for a sign of what his reaction would be. As if reading her mind, his expression grew tender and for a moment, she saw her own pain reflected there.

"Amy is my sister." Her voice cracked. "She was stolen from me."

"Stolen from you?" He abandoned his relaxed posture and straightened. "What about your parents?"

"My mother is dead. My father deserted us when Mama found out she was pregnant with Amy." Annalisa spoke the painful words flatly, reigning in her emotions so she could give Cade only the facts.

Cade pulled a tiny notebook and a pen from his shirt pocket. Flipping the pad open, he made a notation. "How old is Amy?"

"Eight."

"When your mother died she left custody of Amy to you, right?"

"She told me to take care of her." Tears filled her eyes again, as she remembered her mother's last words. "I promised her I would."

Cade reached out and took her hand. "I understand. You're not responsible. When a kidnapping occurs. . ."

The touch of his hand on hers turned her insides to honey. Knowing she needed to be strong, she pulled her hand away and wiped her eyes. "It wasn't exactly a kidnapping."

"What do you mean?" Cade's voice rose. "What exactly was it?"

"Social Services took her from me."

A flicker of shock showed in his eyes, but he quickly resumed his questioning with a poker face. "Why? Do you have a problem? An addiction? Did they find you unfit?"

"They said I was too young."

"Annalisa, that's not logical. Your application to work here said you are twenty-four." Cade discarded the notebook and took her hands in his. "If you have a problem, don't be ashamed to tell me. With God's help, you can overcome your addiction and then maybe we can get Amy back."

Annalisa felt a hysterical laugh bubble up in her throat as she shook her head. "No, Cade. There is no problem. I was only seventeen when they took Amy and put her up for adoption and placed me in foster care."

Cade dropped hold of her hands and stared at her, mouth open. Jumping to his feet, he turned his back on her and strode across the room to the empty fireplace. He stood at the mantle for what seemed an eternity. The loud tick-tock of the grandfather clock echoed through the silent room.

She sat and waited while he picked up pictures and examined them as if he'd forgotten her presence. Suddenly, he spun around.

"This ranch is very important to me. More than you will ever know." He ran his fingers through his hair. "By taking the cook's position, your deception has struck at the heart of my project here." Cade paced up and down in front of the fireplace. "I do feel sorry for you, but there's no way I would ever help you find a little girl who has probably been with another family for seven years. So all you've done is put us both in an impossible situation for nothing."

With each angry word, Annalisa shrank farther into the recliner. The warm honey feeling she'd had earlier rolled into a ball of pain in her chest. He was just like her father. Suave charm and uncontrollable anger all rolled into one.

She had thanked God when her dad left and then cried all night that he was gone. Since then she'd avoided men with any temper. Truthfully, she'd always been so centered on finding Amy, she hadn't had much time for men.

Cade walked over to where she sat. "Please stop looking at me like I'm going to hit you. I would never lay a hand on a woman in anger."

Annalisa found the courage to rise, partly from his reassurance that he wasn't going to strike her. "I'm sorry, Mr. Mc-Fadden, I'll pack tonight and leave first thing in the morning."

"You will not. You're not going anywhere."

five

"What do you mean? You can't possibly want me to stay." Annalisa's voice was incredulous and, just as she'd been doing during their whole conversation, she squeezed the locket around her neck.

What did he mean, Cade wondered. *Why not just let her go?* He motioned her back into her chair. She sat and stared up at him with long, damp lashes. "Look, I hired you to cook, and that's what you're going to have to do. Please. I can't find someone else on such short notice. Two wrongs don't make a right." He shook his head. "You shouldn't have deceived me, but leaving me in a lurch is no way to correct it."

She drew a shuddering breath and met his level gaze. "Okay, then, I'll stay. . .at least until you can find someone else."

"Believe me, I'll call Mrs. Spencer tomorrow and have her start interviewing applicants again. You should be out of here in a couple of weeks." Cade's mind was racing with the unfolding of events of the last hour.

Annalisa sat, without moving, in the easy chair, her face turned away from him. He noticed with irritation her shoulders were, as always, totally erect.

Lord, don't I have a right to be angry?

With obviously fraudulent intent, this woman had managed to jeopardize his new life. Going back to investigating was not a possibility. The boys' ranch had to succeed, or he knew he'd never have peace of mind again. How could it succeed without a cook?

He walked back over to the fireplace, gazing absently at the pictures and mentally running through the possibilities for a temporary chef. He quickly crossed Aunt Gertie off the list. Marta had specified no cooking before she took the job, so he knew that wasn't her forte. Unless George was hiding some great culinary talent, that left Cade.

He could cook a mean breakfast, but other than that, his kitchen expertise was limited to reaching for the phone at the end of the counter to order take-out, something that wasn't available here. Even if they did figure out how to heat microwave dinners, he was pretty sure social services would frown on that menu.

Annalisa would have to stay. These children's lives depended on them being at the ranch. Whether she had any regard for a child's happiness or not, he certainly did.

At that contradictory thought, guilt seized him so suddenly that he pivoted back around to face the recliner, sure she must be glaring at him. Her face was still turned to the wall. She hadn't moved.

His own words had convicted him. Hadn't she been carrying a torch for her sister for seven years, refusing to allow anything to extinguish her flame of hope?

Observing her steadfast profile, he wanted to beg her forgiveness, but he knew nothing would matter to her now, except him agreeing to find her sister. No matter how bad he felt about how he'd treated her, he couldn't do that.

"We'd better call it a night. It's bound to be a long day tomorrow. The boys aren't going to be put off much longer about horseback riding, especially Tim." Cade offered a smile, hoping to erase the harsh words he'd spoken earlier.

"We wouldn't want to disappoint the boys, would we? After all, children matter, don't they, Mr. McFadden?" Each word struck him as if she'd dipped her verbal arrows into his guilt-poisoned conscience and aimed them at the core of his soul.

"Yes, they do."

"The ones who are important to you do anyway. I'd better hurry to bed, so I don't let them down."

"Annalisa. . ." He reached out and touched her arm.

She shook his hand off her arm like it was a snake. "Don't touch me. You'll never know how important this was to me." She gasped back a sob, but fiery sparks seemed to shoot from her brown eyes. "I'll work until you can replace me, then I'll be gone so fast it'll make your head spin." Apparently unable to fight the tears any longer, she almost ran from the room.

He noticed her shoulders were slumped for the first time since he'd met her. Had she really expected him to take on a case that was seven years old and had been entirely legal? Apparently she had.

Her last words lingered in the air. . .*until you can replace me.* He knew Mrs. Spencer could find another cook, but he had a sinking feeling he'd never be able to replace Annalisa Davis.

If he waited a few days to call his office manager, maybe they could work things out. He couldn't find her sister for her, but maybe he could make her realize the futility of trying to change something that happened seven years ago.

He sank down in the recliner, still warm from her body, and wondered what it was about her that fascinated him. Yes, she was beautiful, but he had known countless beautiful women. She was vulnerable, but so was every woman who had walked into his office clutching a picture of a missing child in her hand.

She had an inner strength, as she'd shown tonight by her refusal to give up her quest. Remembering her faith that had gone beyond the terror during the cattle incident, he was humbled. She'd known he'd come to rescue her because she'd prayed he would. Had she prayed he'd help her find her sister? Would she ever understand his refusal?

He'd overheard her with Juan tonight and had been impressed with her apt handling of the teen-ager. She probably would be a fantastic mother. It was a shame she'd been so young when her mother died. Her sister could have done much worse in the parent department.

He slowly stood and walked down the hall, hoping sleep would come quickly. When he heard muffled sobs coming from Annalisa's door he turned to his own room, certain there would be no rest for him tonight.

≥

"Hey, Cade, look at me." Tim grinned at Cade from his position of honor on Old Sweetie's back, while George safely held the reins.

"I'm looking, Tim. You're doing a great job." Cade glanced up at Juan, riding on Bubba. "You doin' okay, Juan?"

"Duh. . .this is stupid kid stuff. I still don't understand why you have to lead me."

Cade met the boy's glittering black eyes with a level gaze. "Juan, I think you need to understand a little about respect. You see, I respect you enough to not want you to get hurt—either your feelings or your backside from falling off a horse. You need to do the same for me, and think before you speak. Hop down now, and let Matthew give it a try."

Their gazes remained locked, but Juan sullenly slid down from the horse. Once on the ground, he averted his eyes and stomped toward the bunkhouse. Cade suppressed a smile. The social worker had warned him the boys would test him to see what they could get by with.

Cade led Bubba to where Matthew stood drawing pictures in the dirt with the toe of his boot. "Matt? Why don't you give it a try, Buddy? Bubba is really gentle."

For the first time, Matthew looked him squarely in the eye. Sorrow washed over Cade as he recognized the combination of overwhelming grief and stark fear. Matthew shook his head, but did reach out and pat Bubba's soft nose, finally burying his little face in the horse's shoulder.

Was this what drove Annalisa to find her sister—the fear that somewhere she was out there walking around with a similar expression? The thought made Cade's blood run cold.

❧

Annalisa watched through the window as Cade coaxed Matthew into patting the horse, then she turned back to the sandwiches. Anger surged through her again as she remembered Cade's harsh words last night. *That man,* she thought, tears welling in her eyes, *his heart is tender to everyone but me.* In spite of her sarcastic words to Cade, her own heart had gone out to these boys, so she could certainly understand his compassion for them. So why couldn't he understand her situation?

She'd expected so much more from him. She fumed as she prepared the simple lunch Cade had requested. This morning he'd been professional, treating her as a respected employee, completely ignoring their earlier exchange concerning Amy.

The sound of the glass doors sliding open and closed was quickly followed by many footsteps. Annalisa frowned as she realized the only boyish voice she heard was Tim's. The other boys were entirely too quiet. If she planned to stay around, even just for two weeks, she'd have to remedy that. She finished slicing the red juicy tomatoes and arranging them on a plate. Right on cue, Aunt Gertie breezed in.

"Oh, my, Hon! Once again you've got it all under control.

Let me help you carry that out." Her sweet voice soothed Annalisa's frazzled nerves, and she gratefully surrendered the platter of meat and cheese. When she followed the older woman out, her gaze flitted to Cade standing at the end of the buffet. She looked away and cast a glance around the room.

Marta smiled and patted the chair beside her. "Come sit down, Annalisa."

"I can't just yet. I still have to get the glasses and tea." Annalisa shook her head as Marta started to rise to help. "No, you stay there and save my seat. I can get them."

When she hurried back into the kitchen, Aunt Gertie had the tray of iced glasses. Annalisa grabbed the pitcher of tea, and they walked out together.

Sliding into the seat Marta had saved, Annalisa bit back a groan. From this spot, every time she looked up from her plate, she would be staring straight at the man she wanted to avoid.

Cade asked George to lead the prayer. As soon as he finished, everyone tackled the sandwiches with enthusiasm. The meal was fairly quiet until Tim burst out, "Oh, no! I lost Buddy!"

"Buddy?" Cade asked.

"My frog." Tears welled up in the boy's eyes. "I put him down on a rock when I was getting ready to ride Bubba, and I forgot to go get him." He swiped his eyes with his sleeve. "I know he'll be gone now."

"I'll help you look for him after lunch," Annalisa offered, sympathy welling up in her heart for the distraught little boy.

"Nah." Cade shook his head. "Buddy's at home right now eatin' lunch with his family. Maybe he'll show up to play again some day, Tim."

The boy looked doubtful. Annalisa's temper flared, and she shot Cade a hard look. "When you lose something important, you look for it."

Cade met Annalisa's gaze with a steely one of his own. "Yes, but sometimes it's better off left lost." Abruptly looking away from her, he turned back to Tim, "That's the way it is with Buddy. He's better off with his family than he would be living in your pocket."

"Perhaps he'd be happier living with Tim, especially since Tim so obviously loves him and would take excellent care of him. Besides, how can we even know his family is around? Maybe they didn't even notice he was missing."

"Regardless, Tim has no right to keep the frog, even if he does love him. Especially if he loves him, he has to think of what's best for Buddy."

"And you think you know what's best?" Annalisa became aware of the other adults' startled expressions, but she couldn't stop. "Why not ask Tim? After all, it's his frog!"

Tim considered this for a minute and then smiled. "Yeah, I guess you're right, Mr. Cade. You don't have to help me look for him, Annalisa. Thanks anyway. He'll come back on his own if he wants to."

Annalisa nodded and returned the boy's smile, but inside she was shaking. Dropping the last half of her sandwich on her plate untouched, she stood. "If y'all will excuse me, I'm going to get an early start on the kitchen."

Cade paused in the kitchen doorway and observed Annalisa as she cleaned the counter. Even with anger radiating from her every move, she was beautiful. She tossed the rag in the sinkful of soapy water, and when she turned around her brown eyes flared with surprise. "Spying on me?"

"No, just watching a master at work." He spoke softly and watched as her stiff posture relaxed. "I thought we might talk."

"Didn't we say it all?" She leaned back against the counter with her arms crossed.

He studied her face and prayed that God would help him find the right words. "Annalisa, I. . .I'm sorry."

Her brown eyes widened. "You've changed your mind? You'll help me find Amy?" Her face, so composed a minute before, broke into a smile that tugged at his heart.

"I'm willing to talk about it more—if you are—and see what we can come up with. I can't go against what I believe is right, but if we both remain rational. . ." He grinned at her to take the sting out of the reminder of their irrational reactions earlier. "I'm sure we can work it out." He cleared his throat. "We do need to discuss it when the boys are not around though. They've had enough turmoil in their lives. Even a simple disagreement like ours in there could cause them to be really upset."

Annalisa lifted her thick hair and held it on top of her head with one hand. Then she looked down and scuffed against the floor with the toe of one sneakered foot. Rubbing the back of her neck with her other hand, she returned his smile with a sheepish one of her own. "I'm sorry. You're right, of course. I guess I overreacted. I've just waited so long to find Amy."

"Truce?" he asked, hoping not to get into a confrontation again while emotions were still high. When she nodded, he continued, "Let's take a break today and talk about it tomorrow, okay? Did I tell you about Old Sweetie giving Juan a big kiss yesterday?"

Relief filled him when Annalisa's sweet laughter resounded in the room.

six

Annalisa leaned in close to the horse's ear and spoke. "Listen, Bubba, you are not going to make me look stupid today. Do you understand?"

Bubba stared back at her with limpid pools of brown. All in all, it was a very noncommittal stare.

Annalisa had more to say, but she cut her equine conversation short when Cade strolled up to her, his grin looking out of place at such an early hour.

"Are you sure you've ridden before?"

Annalisa forced an answering smile. "Yes." She didn't see any point in explaining that she'd been on horseback twice in her life. Once when she was seven her father had surprised her by letting her ride a pony at a traveling carnival. She could still see the fury in his eyes when the attendant had to stop the circular walk to help a terrified Annalisa off. That had been enough to extinguish her girlish fascination with horses.

"Don't you think I should be here to prepare lunch, though? A two hour ride will work up quite an appetite." She shook her head, feigning regret as she gently rubbed the horse's neck. A furtive glance at Cade told her the cowboy definitely wasn't buying her act.

"No, if we're going on the overnight camping trip, we all need to be used to our horses. Since Aunt Gertie's already planned to escape to her sister's that Friday night, she doesn't have to ride today. She said she'd put together some sandwiches

58

while we're gone." He shoved his hat back on his head. "Need any help getting on?"

"No, I'll be fine." She nodded across the pasture toward the small boy struggling valiantly to get up on a chestnut pony. "Looks like Tim could use your help, though."

She breathed a sigh of relief when he hurried over to the boy, leaving her to contemplate her own dilemma.

No matter how soft Bubba's hair felt under her hand, Annalisa knew without a doubt the horse would turn into a bucking, snorting monster once she was astride him.

The idea of being a mile up in the air on an unpredictable beast horrified her. She remembered how she'd tried to explain as much to Julie concerning the trail ride that topped off Family Day at church. Her friend wouldn't take no for an answer.

Annalisa had ended up having a nice long walk in the woods, while she waited for the others to return. It might have been enjoyable if not for her sore behind. Thankfully, the horse, once rid of its unwanted rider, had found its way back to the stables.

She'd thought she'd never have the nerve to climb back on a horse. But, she hadn't figured on Cade McFadden. Since no one was looking, she allowed herself the luxury of watching as his gentle hands lifted Tim into the saddle.

In the last few weeks, she'd come to care about the boys on the ranch, but Cade gave them his heart in everything he did. Unfortunately, every time she mentioned Amy, that soft heart turned to stone.

"We'll talk about it later." That's what he'd said last night when she'd brought it up after supper. She wasn't surprised. Some version of that brush-off was all she'd gotten on the subject since the first day he'd told her they would work something out.

She hadn't heard anything more on him finding a replacement for her either. The two-week deadline had come and gone, but as long as there was a chance he'd help her find Amy, she didn't want to push the issue. Unfortunately, she was afraid he was counting on that. For some reason, it was as if his very life depended on the success of this boys' ranch.

Cade turned abruptly to meet her gaze. Heat crept up her face, and she spun around to Bubba. Without stopping to think it through, she stretched and reached for the saddle horn. Murmuring a quick prayer, she put her left foot in the stirrup and heaved herself up with all her might.

Waves of terror washed over her as she rose high in the air. She squeezed her eyes shut and grabbed at the horse's mane. Her fingers brushed the coarse hair like a taunt as she plummeted to the ground on the opposite side.

~

At the sight of Annalisa flying over Bubba's back, adrenaline shot through Cade's body. He sprinted toward her, fully aware that she would hit the hard ground before he could possibly reach her. Sure enough, she landed with a thud when he was a few feet from her.

"Annalisa! Are you okay?" He started to kneel down beside her, then jerked back in surprise as she sprang to her feet.

"I'm fine." Her face was the color of the jaunty bandanna tied around her neck. "It's been awhile since I've ridden, and I guess I underestimated my arm strength."

Cade frowned, still stuck on her first words. Fine? There was no way she could be fine after a fall like that. "Why don't you take the rest of the day off and go on up to the house?"

She stood straighter. "No, thank you. Like you said, we all need to get used to our horses before the camping trip. I'll just mount more slowly this time."

She bent to brush the dirt from her jeans, and Cade saw a grimace flash across her face. But when she faced him again, it was gone.

Cade took one look at her proud stance and decided to change his tactics. He pasted on a goofy smile. "Excuse me, Ma'am, but that man over there just called me a hundred-pound weakling." He pointed at George, who was, of course, paying no attention to them. "Would you help me prove him wrong by allowing me to assist you in mounting your horse?" He winked at Annalisa. "It would do wonders for my self-esteem."

"Well, if we don't want him to kick sand. . .er. . .dirt in your face, I suppose I'd better."

Rejoicing in her response, even if it was in play, he helped her up on Bubba and pretended not to notice that she trembled. Instead of handing her the reins, he held them in one hand and pointed at the clouds with the other. "Looks like we might be in for some rain."

"Really?" The tremor in her voice told him she was as terrified as he'd suspected. "Soon?"

He bit back a grin at her hopeful tone. "We should have time to get in a little bit of riding."

"Oh. . .good."

He glanced casually around at her, not wanting to give her a reason to get all prickly again. "You know what I just remembered?"

"What?" She was definitely speaking through gritted teeth. He had the feeling that the pain and the terror combined were almost too much for her to bear. Why didn't she just say so?

"I think Bubba does better if you walk him a bit before someone rides him." This was true of all the horses here, since they were usually being ridden by inexperienced riders. Leading the horse was the perfect way to set the rider at ease, as well. But, if she suspected it was for her sake, Cade couldn't see Annalisa agreeing. "Since you're already on, would you mind if I just walk him around with you in the saddle?"

"I suppose that would be fine." Her tone suggested that placing her hand in a hot waffle iron would be preferable, but Cade was pretty sure she considered this the lesser of two evils.

He walked Bubba around the yard as Annalisa held onto the saddle horn with both hands. Halfway around he stopped and looked up at the woman who sat so stiffly. Instead of returning his gaze, she stared at her hands as if willing them not to let go. He glanced back at the boys, who with George and Marta's help, were walking their horses. Making a decision, he led Bubba out of the yard and behind the barn to one of his favorite spots.

Inside a small picket-fenced area, a big oak shaded a wooden swing. Someone, probably his grandmother, had planted roses and other blooming bushes around to make an almost private garden amidst the hustle and bustle of the ranch. A hitching post was conveniently located at the entrance. Cade's grandparents were in Florida now, but it was easy to imagine the romantic couple sitting here watching the sunset.

When he stopped, he looked up to find Annalisa's eyes squeezed shut, her fingers in a death grip on the saddle horn.

"Annalisa. . ." He moved around to the side and touched her leg. She flinched, and he wondered again how bruised she was from her earlier fall. "Let me help you down."

She opened her eyes and offered a defeated nod.

"You did great." He eased her off the horse, taking care not to hurt her.

"Great?" Sarcasm laced her voice, but she didn't jerk her hand away from his, even though she was safe on the ground.

He led her over to the swing, and they sat in silence for a few minutes. "Want to talk about it?"

"About what? My fear of horses?" Tears filled her eyes, and she swiped them away with the back of her hand. "Or the fact that I'm a first-class idiot?"

"Well, let's start with your fear of horses. Why didn't you tell me?" A telltale tear trickled down her cheek, and he reached out to brush it away.

"I wanted to. But I hated to let you down. I've already been such a problem to you, not to mention a disappointment."

He sensed there was more but, in light of their newfound peace, he hated to push. "You may have been a problem at first, but your skills are invaluable here, and you certainly haven't been a disappointment." He stopped himself from telling her how much he'd come to look forward to seeing her every day. "Why did you pretend you weren't hurt from the fall?"

She stared at him for a minute, without answering. Cade had the feeling she was peering into his soul, somehow measuring him. Would she see his darkest secrets? Be privy to his deepest fears? He caught himself silently praying he wouldn't be found lacking.

She dropped her gaze, and as the heavy curtain of brown curls fell down over her face, her voice became muffled. "My dad always taught me to be tough. To show pain is to show weakness, and weakness is unacceptable."

Cade's chest constricted at the words. Hadn't he lived by

that motto himself the last six months? He reached out and eased Annalisa's hair back with his hand. "Honey, weakness is human. We're all weak. Don't you know only God is all powerful?" When had he forgotten that?

"Sure I know that. But knowing doesn't make me forget what I was taught."

"How bad are you hurt?"

"Just bruised." She spoke quietly, still looking down.

"You sure?" He released her hair and tilted her face gently toward him.

Her large brown eyes still shimmered with tears, but she offered a small smile. "Nothing's broken, Cade. Unless you count my pride."

They swung in silence again, but this time the quiet was more companionable. More like Cade could imagine his grandparents sharing. Had God brought Annalisa here for something beyond her own agenda? To his amazement, Cade realized he was at least willing to explore the possibility.

He pushed himself to his feet, then offered his hand to Annalisa. "Pride or no pride, I'll tell you what we're going to do." He pulled her to a standing position. "You're going to march right into that kitchen and get some ice packs out of the freezer. Then you're going to go upstairs to your room and lay down with ice on the sorest spots for at least fifteen minutes."

When she opened her mouth to protest, he held up his hand. "If I sound bossy, there's a very good reason."

She raised her eyebrows in silent question.

"You know the reason." He smiled to take the sting out of his words. "I am the boss."

"I guess I can't argue with that." She flinched as she moved, and he knew she was already stiff. Her smile was genuine though. "Thanks, Cade."

He ushered her out of the little gate and watched as she gingerly walked to the house, then he turned to Bubba with a sigh. "She sure keeps us on our toes, doesn't she, Boy?"

seven

"It's time."

Annalisa dropped the dishrag into the soapy water and spun around to face a smiling Cade. "Time?" She swiped at a stray curl, then immediately regretted it when Cade's grin broadened. "I got soap in my hair, didn't I?"

"Just a little." He stepped forward and gently brushed her hair with his hand.

When he moved back, she was embarrassed to realize she'd been holding her breath. *This isn't a romance novel,* she mentally chided herself. Why had she gone weak in the knees half expecting him to kiss her?

She bit her lip and met his scrutinizing gaze. "Time for what?"

"Your first official lesson with Bubba."

Her knees stayed weak, but all thought of kisses fled from her mind. "Cade, I can't."

"Yes, you can. The dishes are done. It's the perfect time."

"That's not what I mean, and you know it." She glowered at him, but his grin never faltered.

"Run up and get ready. I'll be waiting at the barn."

"But, Cade—"

"Hurry." The last word drifted back as he let the door close behind him.

Annalisa had a feeling if she didn't hurry, Cade would be back to throw her over his shoulder and tote her out to the horse like a sack of potatoes. With that embarrassing image branded on her mind, she rushed to her room to change.

Ten minutes later, she emerged into the sunny day and started for the barn.

"Annalisa! Over here." Cade waved from the open door of the bunkhouse, and she redirected her steps.

"Come in for a sec and see what Marta has done." Cade stepped back and allowed her to enter.

When her eyes adjusted to the light, she grinned. "Marta, you've worked wonders here."

The older woman blushed, but Annalisa could tell she was pleased with the well-deserved compliment.

Marta had given the bunkhouse an amazingly homey touch. Matching blankets covered the boys' beds and the tan couch was adorned with coordinating pillows. Beside each bed, small braided rugs stood out against the shiny hardwood floors.

"Did you do all this by yourself?" Annalisa asked, her eyes taking in the log walls tastefully decorated with Native American art.

Before Marta could answer, George stepped through the doorway. "She sure did. A neighbor gave her some goose feathers, and she even hand-stuffed the pillows." His pride was so obvious it almost hurt Annalisa to see it. What would it be like to have a husband so admiring? Her father's compliments to her mother had always prefaced some favor he needed.

"Cade, Bubba's ready." George's words brought her back to the present with a jolt.

Bubba may be ready, but Annalisa's not. Annalisa bit back the caustic comment and followed Cade wordlessly out of the cabin. When they'd walked a few steps, he gave her ponytail a gentle tug.

"Get that scared look off your face, Girl. Don't you know I'm not going to let anything hurt you if I can help it?"

"If that were really true, you'd help me find Amy." Annalisa said the words without thinking, but the pain in Cade's expression pricked her conscience. Before she could apologize for her outspokenness, Tim approached, leading Bubba.

"Here you go, Mr. Cade. They're all done except him." He handed the reins to Cade.

Cade doffed his hat at the boy and motioned for Annalisa to follow him into the barn.

When they stopped, she gritted her teeth and closed her eyes for a moment of silent prayer.

"Here."

She braced herself and opened her eyes. To her surprise, instead of the reins, Cade handed her a brush.

"What's this for?"

"Bubba's had his morning ride. Now it's time for grooming."

"I'm supposed to groom him?"

"That's the general idea." Cade's smile returned. "I thought it would be better for you to get used to him on the ground at first."

Relief flooded her, and she had to restrain herself from throwing her arms around the thoughtful cowboy.

Thirty minutes later, Annalisa was tired, but her spirit had lightened. Cade had gotten her started on grooming Bubba, then gone off to check on the boys.

Even brushing the big animal had terrified Annalisa at first, but the horse had so obviously enjoyed the attention that she'd soon calmed down.

"That wasn't so bad, was it?" Cade asked from the doorway of the barn.

"No. But that doesn't mean he won't throw me off again if I get on him."

The corners of Cade's mouth twitched, and Annalisa glared

at his obvious attempt to contain his amusement.

"Okay, so maybe he didn't exactly throw me off. . . ," she conceded reluctantly.

Cade snorted, then broke out in laughter, the deep sound resonating through the barn. "If you could have seen yourself. . ." He collapsed on the barstool and swiped at his eyes. "I don't think Bubba moved one inch. When you flew over his back, he must have thought. . ."

His gasping hilarity proved contagious and in spite of herself, Annalisa felt mirth bubbling up. Soon, she was leaning against the wall of Bubba's stall, laughing so hard she could barely breathe.

"He must have thought I was a lunatic," Annalisa finished for Cade when she could speak again.

"I'm sorry. It wasn't remotely funny then, but now that you're all healed up and claiming poor Bubba threw you off. . ." Cade grinned. "It's been too long since I've laughed. I've forgotten how good it feels."

"Yeah, me too. Thanks for starting it, even if it was at my expense." Annalisa gathered her courage. "What happened to make you lose the laughter in your life, Cade? I told you my secrets. Now it's your turn."

As the emotions played across his chiseled face, she thought he wasn't going to answer. But he motioned her to grab a stool from its resting place against the wall.

She took the seat and settled it next to his.

"As you know. . ." He raised one eyebrow sardonically. ". . .my office sort of specializes in finding missing children."

"Yes, you have a knack for that kind of investigation. I wondered why you gave it up."

"I always considered that knack a blessing, really, until lately. I can think like a kidnapper and follow a trail that everyone else sees as cold. But last year. . ." His expression grew pensive, and he stared at the tack hanging on the wall as if seeing something she couldn't.

"Last year, a woman hired me to find her four-year-old son. Her ex-husband had taken him and fled to parts unknown. She was desperate to get her boy back, and I was eager to help. Abductions by non-custodial parents are fairly common, but that doesn't stop the heartache that comes with it."

He turned to look at Annalisa. She nodded, afraid if she spoke, he'd stop.

"Everything went smoothly, a routine investigation, really." He shook his head. "People are creatures of habit. The boy's father loved baseball. I knew the general area in Florida he favored. All that was left was to watch the T-ball teams."

Annalisa nodded, puzzled. "It sounds like you did a great job."

Cade laughed, but the contrast between this cynical chuckle and his earlier gleeful laugh sent pain shooting through Annalisa's heart. Whatever had happened had wounded this gentle man deeply.

"The mother thought so. She was thrilled to have her son back. The boy. . . Well, the poor little guy was unsure how to feel. He loved his mama and his daddy. In a perfect world he could have had them both."

Cade stopped speaking, and the silence stretched between them so loud it echoed off the rafters of the old barn. The morning sun shone through the big door, and Annalisa thought she saw a hint of moisture in Cade's eyes.

Dear Lord, please help him to heal of this great pain. Give him courage to overcome the past.

Cade swallowed loudly. "The father was arrested by the local police and held for questioning. They didn't realize how upset he was at losing his only son. Needless to say, they were shocked to find him hanging in his cell."

"Oh, Cade."

He looked up at her, and the deep emotion in his eyes shook her to the core. "I have pictures of them laughing together, Annalisa. Photos of a loving father teaching his son how to hold the bat, how to position his glove."

"But that wasn't his right. . ."

"What made me the judge and jury? Maybe the courts were wrong. Maybe the child would have been happy with his father." He lifted his cowboy hat off his head. His next words were spoken so softly she had to lean forward to hear them. "Nothing I can do will ever make that little boy's life any better. I killed his father."

Annalisa slid off the stool and put her hand on Cade's arm. He looked up at her and she put her arms around him. They embraced in silence, while Annalisa prayed for words of comfort.

"Cade, you did your job. He broke the law, and he knew the risk of getting caught. That was his choice. And you know what else? He could have gotten a lawyer and fought. But he chose to take his own life." She pulled back and met his troubled gaze. "What if he had gotten laid off or something down the road and decided to commit suicide then? What if his son had found him? You don't know what the future held for them and because of his actions—not yours—no one ever will."

"Thanks. I know you're trying to make me feel better. But I know what I have to do. If I can use this ranch and make a difference in these boys' lives and in the lives of others like them, it won't make up for what happened to Joey's dad, but maybe I'll be able to have peace." He stared at the ceiling as if searching for the words. "Two things I know—I can't allow this ranch to fail. And I'll never ever be responsible for taking a child out of a home they're happy in."

Biting back the tears at this unbelievable impasse they'd reached, she nodded to show her understanding of his position.

"I'm sorry I can't help you, Annalisa. All I can do is pray that God gives you peace." He reached out and brushed an errant curl away from her face. "But I will tell you a secret. I'm awfully glad He brought you to Circle-M ranch."

Annalisa's knees went rubbery again, and it had nothing to do with horses. Life wasn't a romance novel, but he was definitely going to kiss her. Even though he'd just gently crushed her hope, she was helpless to resist the feelings she had for him. As he lowered his mouth to hers, she admitted something she'd been fighting the last few weeks. She was falling in love with Cade McFadden.

"Cade?" Before their lips touched, George's voice caused them to jerk apart.

They glanced toward the doors as the man entered the barn. "What can I do for you, George?" Cade asked.

"It's Tim. I think he's having an asthma attack. He's having trouble breathing."

eight

Cade dashed out of the barn, with George close at his heels. Annalisa hurried after them. Breathing hard from her unexpected sprint, she reached the bunkhouse only seconds after the men.

Tim sat on the sofa, with Marta kneeling in front of him. She looked up when they walked in. "Since he used the inhaler, he's breathing much better."

Cade strode across the room and sat down beside Tim. "Hey, Bud. You doing all right?"

"Yeah, I think so." Tears still lingered in the little boy's eyes, and his voice had a slightly wheezy tone. "I didn't think I was going to have asthma since I moved here. It's been a long time since I had an attack."

Annalisa watched in admiration as Cade put his arm gently around Tim's shoulders and spoke reassuringly. "That's a really good thing, Tim. Probably the attacks are getting further and further apart, and pretty soon, they'll stop altogether. We can handle a little one like this now and then, can't we?"

"You're not mad?" Tim looked up at Cade, and Annalisa's heart broke at what the child must have gone through before becoming a ward of the state.

Cade smiled gently. "Mad? No way. Tim, if I cut my hand or banged my head, would you be mad at me?"

"No." Tim still looked uncertain.

"I'll never be mad at you for being sick either." Cade looked at George, Marta, and Annalisa and nodded. "None of us will be."

"That's good, because I really can't help it." Tim's fears were relieved, but Annalisa sensed he still felt the need to defend his illness. Anger rose in her at his parents.

"Tim?" She stepped forward.

"Yes, Ma'am?"

"I heard something making a funny noise under the porch this morning. It almost sounded like kittens."

"Kittens?" His eyes widened.

"Yep. If it's okay with Mr. Cade, why don't you go tell Juan and Matthew and meet back at the porch to see if we can figure it out."

"Sure!" He jumped up and walked to the door. Just before he reached the threshold, he screeched to a stop. "Oops." He turned back to Cade. "Is it okay?"

"Definitely." Before the word was out of Cade's mouth, Tim scampered out the door.

Cade smiled at Annalisa. "Good diversion." His tone grew serious. "We're all going to have to work on assuring Tim that his illness isn't his fault."

"It breaks my heart to see him think that," Marta said.

George nodded. "Like Cade said, it's up to us to change his thinking."

"Maybe some old-fashioned puppy love will help. Well, in this case, kitten love." Annalisa laughed. "I really did hear something that sounded like kittens under the porch, and I've been seeing Miss Kitty go under there a lot," she said. "Y'all want to go out and see what we can find?"

"Sounds like a plan," Cade agreed.

George and Marta nodded and walked out on the porch.

Cade swept his arm gallantly toward the door. "After you," he said to Annalisa, a smile softening his chiseled features.

She stepped in front of him and hurried out, trying to

ignore the undercurrents that ran between them like a raging river.

Tim ran up the path to the porch, while Juan and Matthew followed behind at a slower gait. Even the blasé teenager couldn't keep the interest from showing in his expression, and Annalisa noticed Matthew was making eye contact rather than staring at the ground.

Please, Lord, it would be so nice if there were kittens underneath the porch.

To Annalisa's surprise, Matthew was the first one to plop down on his stomach and shimmy under the porch. She looked at Cade and mouthed, "Is it safe?"

He nodded and whispered, "We added the porch right before you got here. I don't think it's been here long enough to attract any dangerous varmints." But as soon as he finished speaking, he squatted down and peered into the darkness.

"Are those kittens, Matt?"

Silence.

"Matthew?"

The boy squirmed, and it was obvious he wanted to reply. Annalisa breathed a silent prayer, but instead of a verbal answer, Matthew wiggled out into the light and held up three kittens. He cuddled a gray tiger-striped one close, but silently pushed the other two toward Tim.

Tim whooped. At the loud noise the two loose little kittens scampered back toward the porch, but the boy caught them. "Here, Juan." He extended the Siamese-looking kitten, keeping a calico for himself.

Annalisa noticed Cade was watching to see if Juan would accept the gift. When, after a moment's hesitation, the teen reached for the wriggling bundle of fur, they exchanged a smile.

"Is it okay if we play with them awhile?" Tim asked.

"Considering they have their eyes open and are fairly agile, I'd say they're old enough to handle a little gentle play." Cade stressed the word gentle. "Miss Kitty's probably still out at the barn, but I imagine she'll be getting ready to feed them again soon. Let's limit it to ten minutes, then they go back to their home, okay?"

His gaze scanned the three boys' faces. They all nodded, then as if by unspoken agreement, walked away in different directions for some quality time with their new feline friends. "I'll ring the dinner bell when time is up," Cade called after them.

"That was amazing, seeing them so excited, wasn't it?" George mused.

"Did you see Juan?" Marta asked. "I'm pretty sure that was a positive emotion on his face."

"And Matthew almost talked," Annalisa noted. "Didn't you think so, Cade?"

"It sure looked that way."

"Wow." Marta grinned. "Maybe we should have taken that weekend seminar in animal therapy, George."

"I don't know. I think we're hobbling along pretty well on our own."

"You don't think Tim is allergic to cats, do you?" Annalisa hated to put a damper on the positive atmosphere, but the nagging question begged to be voiced.

Cade looked concerned, but Marta shook her head. "He's been playing with Miss Kitty ever since he got here and no attacks until today. So, I really don't think so."

"We'll keep an eye on him and see if his breathing problems worsen now that the kittens are around," George offered. "While I've got a minute to myself, I'm going to go fix that loft ladder out at the barn. If I see the proud mama out there, I'll try to delay her so the young 'uns can play a while longer." He whistled a cheery tune as he made his way down the pathway.

Marta smiled at Cade and Annalisa from the bunkhouse door. "I've got things to do, as well. I'm going to get back in here. Give me a yell if you need me."

Annalisa suddenly found herself alone with Cade on the big porch. He pointed at the swing. "Have a seat."

She sat down and tensed when he eased down beside her.

"You don't have to be so uncomfortable with me. I was going to kiss you back there—not bite you."

"Whew. That's a relief," she said. Her attempt at silly was falling flat, but she couldn't seem to help it. "I was afraid I'd wandered into a bad vampire movie."

"Annalisa—"

"Cade—"

"You go first," Annalisa said, her resolve weakening already.

"I think I'm falling in love with you."

Her mouth went dry. She hadn't expected him to address the situation so directly. "I have to find Amy." She offered the words almost matter-of-factly. "Until I do, I have no future." She turned in the swing to face him. "I promised."

"Annalisa. . ." His voice was as smooth as a chocolate latte. She couldn't help but remember all the times her dad had charmed her mom with a tone much like Cade's present one. ". . .Amy has a future already. It's just not with you." He leaned back in the swing and put one arm around her. She felt sure he was working at looking relaxed. "I've watched you with the boys." He reached out and brushed a stray curl from her face. "You don't have a selfish bone in your body."

"Wanting to raise my baby sister isn't selfish." She refused to be swayed by his soft words.

"No, it isn't. But taking her away from a place where she's happy so you can have her for yourself is."

"How do you know she's happy? Do you know where she is?" Her pulse quickened as she realized he might.

"No." He reached for her hand, but she jerked it away. "I'm sorry. I don't."

Hopes dashed, Annalisa leapt to her feet. "I'm going to find her, Cade. With or without you."

He wouldn't meet her gaze, but glanced instead at his watch. "I've got to ring the bell so the boys will bring the kittens back."

"I'm going for a walk."

Annalisa set off for the barn lot as the dinner bell rang. She needed some time to think. From Cade's reaction and his confession in the barn, she surmised he'd never intended to help her find Amy. He was no different than her father. He'd needed her to cook, and so he pretended he might locate her little sister. Now that he knew she couldn't be put off much longer, he'd tried a different tactic—claiming he was falling in love with her. No doubt hoping to make her forget about finding Amy.

Even as the bitter thoughts tumbled through her mind, Annalisa knew she was being ridiculous. Cade had never promised to help her. He'd only said they'd talk about it. And they just had.

She glanced over at the hay barn where George's hammering resounded through the loft, then headed for the horse barn farther down the path. The Winemillers were sweet, but she knew they hoped she and Cade would get together. No matter how well-meaning, she didn't need advice from either of them right now.

She had a sickening feeling that Cade hadn't been manipulating her when he'd said he was falling in love with her. And an equally sickening feeling that she was way too close to returning his affection.

Just as she reached the barn, Miss Kitty sauntered out. Cade had apparently rung the bell just in time. The feline mommy wouldn't have been too happy to find no kittens under the porch.

When Annalisa entered the broad doorway, in spite of her tumultuous thoughts, she couldn't keep from chuckling at the fact that she zeroed in on Bubba. How quickly her mortal enemy had become her friend.

Once inside, she leaned against the rough boards of Bubba's stall and reached out a trembling hand to pet the horse. "What have I done, Old Boy? It wasn't supposed to be like this."

Bubba put his nose in her open palm and snorted gently against her hand.

"Yeah, I know you think things are going great. But your master is a distraction I can't afford."

Bubba didn't answer, but he turned his head away from her.

"Fine." Feeling more than a little silly, Annalisa turned to walk out of the barn.

Before she reached the doorway, a loud whinny broke the silence. She spun around to see Bubba craning his head over the top of his stall.

"Now you want to reconsider, huh, you big old galoot? Sorry for ignoring me?" She retraced her steps and patted him. "I don't blame you for thinking I'm crazy. Sometimes I wonder myself." She closed her eyes and laid her head against the horse's shoulder.

A picture of the cowboy she'd left on the bunkhouse porch filled her mind's eye. "Cade's everything I've ever dreamed of in a man," she said softly. "But if I settle down to life here, I'm breaking a promise I've spent the last seven years trying to keep."

Annalisa drew a little comfort from the fact that this time the horse turned his head and nuzzled her. Now if only Cade could understand as easily.

nine

From his vantage point on the hill, Cade reined in Duke and looked out over the lush green land that had been in the McFadden family for generations. When Cade's mother and father had married, Jeb, anxious to prove his independence, had bought his own ranch about eighty miles southwest.

Cade had been raised there, but something about this place was in his blood. His grandparents had spent most of their lives here—loving each other and loving the land.

Last year, they'd decided to move to Florida, in hopes that a warmer climate would help his grandmother's arthritis. Cade had known they were afraid they were going to have to break the family tradition and sell the land to someone other than a McFadden. So, even though they were worried about their oldest grandson, he knew they'd been thrilled when he had leased the farm and house to start a boys' ranch.

Since he'd come to live on his grandparents' ranch, the years he spent in Little Rock seemed almost as if they'd never happened. The idea of going back permanently held no appeal. Instead he found himself thinking more and more of making a home here. He was growing closer to the boys every day.

And then there was Annalisa. Her easy laugh and caring nature had become as much a part of the ranch as his grandmother's roses. She'd stolen his heart, but she hadn't spoken to him since their conversation on the porch yesterday. She'd shoved aside his confession of love to bring the focus back on her quest. Even though he couldn't help but admire her single-mindedness, disappointment swept over him again.

Cade's gaze caught activity a little farther down the fence line. He followed the movement to a family of rabbits enjoying an early morning clover feast. He sighed. If only his brown-haired beauty could understand the probable heartbreak of finding her little sister and trying to take her from her family.

Amy had undoubtedly been adopted by now, and Annalisa wouldn't have a legal leg to stand on. The result of such an investigation would be devastating to all involved—the kind of devastation Cade had seen firsthand.

⁂

Annalisa gripped the reins tightly and tried to respond to Cade's encouraging smile. She'd thought about not coming, but had reconsidered. Giving up wasn't her style. So, she'd sat carefully astride Bubba as Cade led them around and around the corral, then had accepted the reins when he'd offered. Now as she completed her first time around by herself, he gave her a big thumbs-up.

She eased the reins into one hand and returned his gesture, cautiously optimistic as a result of this minor success. Bubba hadn't shrunk, but Cade's slow-paced lessons had paid off. She wasn't as intimidated by either Bubba's size or his "horsiness" in general as she once had been.

"Want to pick up the pace a little?" Cade yelled from the fence.

"Not really." She shook her head so vigorously that she felt the clip give way, and her hair tumbled down her shoulders. "Oops." She emitted a nervous giggle.

"It's up to you, but he'll go at a very gentle trot."

"How do I do that?"

"Ease up on the reins a little and give him his head. He likes to trot."

Annalisa stopped pulling so hard on the reins, and Bubba slowly picked up a little speed. *This isn't so unpleasant.*

If only her hands weren't cramping from holding so tightly. She glanced at her white knuckles, but looked up again quickly as she caught sight of the ground speeding by.

"Cade, how do I stop?"

"Pull back on the reins and say, 'Whoa!' "

"Whoa!" Annalisa called as she yanked the reins back. Bubba came to a halt so abruptly she thought she'd go over his head like a cartoon character. "Whoa. . ." she repeated, slightly dazed.

"Good brakes," Cade offered as he walked up to take the reins from her. "You did great today, Anna Banana."

"I did, didn't I?" Even though she was still a little shaken by her sudden stop, she couldn't help but feel a little giddy at her success. Maybe that was why the nickname she'd hated in school sounded like an endearment coming from Cade's lips.

"Tomorrow, you can ride down to the river and back." He nodded to the small river that sluiced through the land about a half mile from the house.

"Only if you ride Duke and go with me."

"I'd love to." His inscrutable expression unnerved her. "I wasn't sure I'd be welcome."

"I'm sorry. I know I overreacted yesterday." She carefully slid off Bubba. "I guess it's a sensitive subject for me."

"I understand."

"I'd better take Bubba and groom him. Same time, same place?" she asked.

"Sounds good."

She turned to lead Bubba toward the barn.

"Hey, Annalisa. . ."

She spun around to face him.

"How about we get an early start tomorrow? There's something I'd like to show you."

"Sure. How early?"

"Five thirty?"

She almost gasped, but squared her shoulders and grinned. "Sure. See you then."

⁂

"I need to be back in an hour so I can take a shower and have breakfast ready at eight," Annalisa called to Cade across the barn lot.

Dressed in a crisp, short-sleeved cotton shirt and a pair of faded denim jeans, she looked as fresh as if she'd spent hours getting ready. If it hadn't been for her groggy reply when he'd knocked on her door fifteen minutes ago, he'd have never guessed she'd thrown herself together.

Of course, he mused, she looked better thrown together than most women he'd ever known after hours of beauty routines. Even early in the morning, she carried herself with the grace of a queen, her head held high and, as usual, her shoulders back. Her thick brunette curls were pinned atop her head and a smattering of freckles wound their way across her well-defined nose.

In the semi-darkness of early morning, her gaze met his. "I have the horses saddled and ready," he said, surprised by the sudden awkwardness he felt. "We should have plenty of time."

He watched in admiration as she mounted Bubba with no difficulty. She'd progressed quickly over the last few days. He'd never taught a more determined student. With a nod to her, he settled his hat firmly on his head, jumped on Duke, and led the way.

"Slow down," Annalisa called.

"Sorry." Cade eased his horse to a trot and noted with satisfaction that she quickly caught up with him.

When they reached the riverbank, he slid to the ground and extended a hand to help her down from Bubba.

The horses, content to graze, stayed where they were while Cade carefully assisted Annalisa down the dimly lit footpath to the river.

"What are we doing?" she asked.

"Shh. . .the show's about to start." He sat down and motioned her to do the same.

"The show?" Her tone was puzzled, but she followed his example and sank onto the dewy grass.

He leaned toward her and pointed to a large break in the trees across the river. He smiled when Annalisa caught her breath in wonder.

Tiny fingers of light stretched up to meet the new day, rising over the craggy skyline. Explosions of brightness extended out to the gray morning sky, ending in streaks of pink and orange. Slowly, a huge ball of yellow light ascended from the vee of the two hills coming together.

"The heavens declare the glory of God," Cade whispered.

"And the firmament showeth his handiwork," Annalisa murmured.

They sat, motionless, until the sun was completely raised and a beautiful blue curtain had pushed back the gray.

"Thanks." Annalisa cleared her throat and, when he looked at her, he noticed her eyes were moist. "I needed that." She spoke softly in the quiet of the newborn day. "I constantly tell myself God is in control, but a physical reminder helps."

"Same here." Cade marveled that their thoughts could run so completely parallel. Most people would have probably raved about the undeniable beauty of the sunrise, but both of them—

a beautiful woman obsessed with her loss and a man haunted by guilt—had seen the power of God, first and foremost.

He rose and offered a hand to Annalisa.

She allowed him to pull her to her feet. "Puts everything into perspective, doesn't it?"

"That's why I come down here." He started down the path with her by his side.

"And why you wanted to bring me?" Annalisa gave him a wry smile. "You think I need perspective?"

"The thought had crossed my mind," Cade said, guiding her to the horses.

When they reached the animals, he turned to face her and brought his other hand around so that both his hands spanned her waist. "Annalisa, I meant what I said the other day on the porch."

"I know. I. . ." Conflicting emotions shone in her luminous brown eyes, and he found himself desperately wanting to kiss the confusion away.

"You don't have to say anything," Cade interrupted her. His gaze lingered on her lips but he dropped a chaste kiss on her forehead and released her.

When he was on Duke's back, he noticed she was still standing by Bubba. "You coming?"

"Yeah," she said, almost absently, as she climbed up in the saddle. "I'll have to hurry to get breakfast."

ten

Annalisa sprinkled the shredded cheese on the skilletful of scrambled eggs then grabbed a fork to turn the bacon. She'd gotten a late start on breakfast, but the sunrise had been worth this frantic preparation.

Only one thing about the morning bothered her. Sharing such a beautiful example of God's power had shaken the wall she'd erected between herself and Cade McFadden. Her resolve to maintain a distance from him was crumbling. She'd bitten her tongue this morning to keep from admitting her own feelings. She knew him. Once he realized how much she cared about him, he'd stop at nothing to keep her here.

Staring absently at the frying bacon, she slumped against the counter. An almost physical weariness spread across her shoulders. For seven long years, she'd held her promise to Amy sacred, refusing to let anyone or anything dissuade her from her task. Now, a devastatingly handsome cowboy threatened to make her forget.

She'd already compromised her convictions by staying here. He wasn't the only private investigator in the world. As soon as she'd known for sure he wouldn't help her find Amy, she should've moved on to find someone who would. Instead she'd allowed herself to become needed here, to grow close to the boys, and to fall in love with Cade.

The outside door opened to reveal the man who had been dominating her thoughts. She pulled herself up to her full height and, forcing a smile to her lips, she nodded. "Cade."

He returned her nod with a grin. "Annalisa."

"Where are the others?"

"George just got back from transporting our overnight gear to the campsite. Now he and the boys are packing the horses. Marta's supervising. Did Aunt Gertie get off okay?"

"Yes, she left about an hour ago. She said y'all had already said your good-byes."

He nodded. "I know she likes it here, but I bet the peace and quiet of Aunt Ruth's house will be a nice treat."

"I don't know. She held onto my hand like she didn't want to let go," Annalisa said as she eased the bacon on to the paper-towel-topped plate.

"I can understand that."

It took a minute for her to grasp his meaning. She quickly looked up to meet his gaze. His blue eyes had grown dark and serious.

A sudden burning sensation brought her attention back to her cooking. She grabbed her hand. "Ouch!"

"Here." Cade switched off the burner and shepherded Annalisa to the sink. He kept one arm around her while he turned the cold water tap on, then gently guided her hand under the soft stream. "Hold that right there."

When he released her, a bereft feeling almost overwhelmed her, even though he only took two steps away. He opened the corner lazy Susan and pulled out the aloe-vera gel.

"It'll be okay. It's only a little place where a splatter of hot grease got me." She held her hand out to show him the red spot.

"Just hush." He popped the top and squirted some green gel on his fingertips. "I need you in good shape to cook for this trip, otherwise the rest of us won't be able to keep our energy up." Teasing glints sparkled in his blue eyes, but he took her hand and cradled it in his as tenderly as if it were a baby.

She watched, mesmerized, as he dabbed the cool gel on the burn and then rubbed the excess into her palm.

"Thanks." She cleared her throat and pulled her hand back. "It'll be as good as new. You'll be happy to know y'all won't starve now."

He transferred his hand to her cheek and lightly caressed it with his thumb. "You know that was my big worry, don't you?"

The back door banged open and Annalisa jumped.

"Mr. Cade! Mr. Cade! Mr. George broke his leg!" Tim's high-pitched voice demonstrated his distress, and tears streamed down his face.

Cade ran out the door, but Annalisa grabbed Tim and pulled him close. His bony shoulders shook under his sweaty shirt as he buried his head in her waist.

"Whoa, Timbo. Hang on a minute. Let's just think about this. Even if Mr. George's leg is broken, he'll be okay. And you won't do him any good if you get too upset."

"You don't understand," Tim wailed. He pulled his face away and looked up at her. Her heart broke as she saw the little tear trickle highways of clean skin on his dirty face. "It was my fault! I'm the one who made him fall."

❧

Beside the porch, George writhed on the ground, holding his ankle. Marta bent over him, and her concerned expression lent impetus to Cade's strides as he ran to them.

"How bad is it?"

"It's sprained," George grunted. "Trick ankle."

"An old football injury," Marta explained to Cade, but her gaze never left her husband's pale face.

Cade squatted down beside them. "How did it happen?"

"I'm so clumsy, that's how. I tripped and fell off the porch."

"You had stuff in front of you and couldn't see where you

were going. . ." Marta jumped to her husband's defense.

"How can you know it's just sprained?" Cade slipped George's boot off and warily eyed the purplish blue ankle. "I think you need a second opinion."

George pushed up to a sitting position. "No. We're headin' out shortly. I'm not going to let the boys down."

Marta sat down beside him. "George." She shook her head, and Cade could see she was struggling not to throttle her husband.

"Annalisa and I will do just fine with the boys overnight. We may not be able to teach them everything you could, but they'll still have a good time." He gave the big man a reassuring grin. "I know almost every verse of most campfire songs. What I don't know, she'll fill in."

Cade couldn't believe he'd begun to think of them as a team, but his heart swelled with the rightness of it.

Marta gave George a hard look, and he finally nodded. "I guess it wouldn't hurt to let the doctor have a look at it." His wife rewarded him with a sweet smile.

"It doesn't do any good to argue with them," George said with a wry grin. "You might as well remember that with Annali—oomph!"

Cade had thought he'd imagined seeing Marta's elbow digging into George's ribs, but George gave his side an exaggerated rub and glared at her.

"We'd better get you to the doctor, Hop-a-long," Marta said, helping George to one foot and supporting his weight on the other side.

"Here, I'll help." Cade reached out, but Marta shooed him away.

"No, you've got your hands full. I can handle George. We'll be here when you get back from camping."

"Did you see the hospital sign when you came through Pocahontas?"

The couple exchanged a significant look and laughed aloud. Apparently noticing Cade's puzzled expression, George explained. "I pointed it out when we came through town. I told Marta that with these three boys, we'd better know where the local ER is because it's a cinch they'll end up there. Now look who's the first one to take advantage of the medical facilities."

Cade was still chuckling at George's good attitude as he watched them hobble out to the van and awkwardly load in.

Suddenly he realized someone was missing. Two someones to be exact—Juan and Matthew. They were supposed to have been helping George pack the horses.

He walked in the back door to the kitchen where Annalisa perched on a low stool with Tim on her knee. He had his head buried in her shoulder. She was smoothing his hair and talking to him in low tones. She looked up when Cade strode in and offered a poignant smile as she cuddled the child.

When had they started knowing what the other one was thinking? He could tell Amy filled her thoughts.

"How's George?" she asked, her voice low.

Tim sat up and turned to Cade, obviously anxious to hear the answer.

"He's okay. 'Trick ankle,' he said. I made him go get it checked out anyway."

"Tim thought it was his fault George got hurt," Annalisa said.

"His fault?" Cade stared at the child whose bottom lip had started trembling again. "How could it be his fault?"

"Apparently George had his arms full and hadn't noticed Tim was in front of him. He tripped over Tim and fell off the porch."

"Timbo. . ." Cade knelt down in front of Annalisa and touched Tim's arm. "Son, you know George didn't blame you. He said it was an accident. What if you'd been the one who'd gotten hurt. Would you have blamed him for falling on you?"

Tim shook his head, his wide eyes still full of tears, but not overflowing. "Now we won't get to go camping today, will we?"

"Well, that all depends," Cade drawled, rising to his feet. "We will if you can find your two cabin mates."

"Juan and Matthew?" Tim's excitement caused his sadness to abate. "George sent them out behind the barn to dig fishing worms. He said all we could have for supper is what we catch ourselves." Tim slid off Annalisa's knee and regarded her solemnly. "Otherwise, how will we ever be able to take care of ourselves in the woods?"

"How about you go see how many worms they've found? And tell them I'm going to need help loading things," Cade said.

"Sure!" Tim hurried out the door, as always letting the screen door slam shut behind him.

&

Annalisa had trouble believing she was really riding along on a horse, relaxed, and enjoying the beautiful day. The cowboy with the knee-weakening grin beside her was icing on the cake. The three boys up ahead didn't look relaxed, but at least they weren't falling off.

"Do you think George's ankle is broken?" she asked.

"No. In spite of Tim's melodramatic claim, I think it's only sprained."

"You think Tim was trying to get attention?"

"No!" Cade held the reins in one hand and took off his Stetson with the other. He readjusted it back on. "I don't think that at all. But, didn't that seem odd to you—Tim getting so upset about George's fall and thinking he'd caused it?" Cade asked.

She cast a sideways glance at him. "Not really. Sometimes people take responsibility for things like that. Even if it's not their fault, they think it is."

"Is that your official opinion?" Cade stared straight ahead, as if the trail was of great interest.

"Could be."

"Sometimes things really are the person's fault and taking responsibility is a release."

"I'm sure you're right about that, but I'd still say that more often than not, especially when other people can see objectively, but the person involved can't, they aren't responsible for what happened."

"Why would someone want to take responsibility for a bad thing if it wasn't true?"

"Sometimes people can't recognize the truth." Annalisa sneaked another peek at his chiseled profile. "Especially when they've held onto a lie for so long."

"I'd better ride up and check on the boys." Cade prodded Duke on and quickly left Annalisa and Bubba alone on the trail.

She leaned forward and patted the side of Bubba's neck. "I'll eventually convince him. You just wait and see." As she stared out at the beautiful rolling hills, she thought about the implications of the word 'eventually.' The temptation to snuggle in and nest at the Circle-M was overpowering. After all the rundown rental houses her family had lived in, followed by years of being a guest, albeit a cherished one, in Julie's home, didn't she deserve a place she could belong? Unfortunately, she'd never belonged anywhere like she did in Cade's arms.

Disgusted by her selfish thoughts, she edged Bubba up to a trot. Amy had just as much right to a loving home as she did.

Annalisa could find her sister and reclaim her without Cade's help. Then once she had custody, they would come back here.

Would Cade accept her if he knew she'd taken Amy away from someone? Knowing how strongly he felt about it, he might not. But that was a chance she'd have to take. She wouldn't ruin the camping trip, but as soon as they got back to the house, she'd give Cade her two weeks' notice. Amy's happiness was worth it.

❧

The bass pond on the back of the nine-hundred-acre ranch wasn't as crystal clear as some of the spring-fed ponds scattered around the property. The boys, especially Juan, had snarled up their noses at the green-skimmed water.

They weren't snarling anymore.

"I got a big one this time!" Juan's unadulterated joy rang out across the water.

Cade and Annalisa shared another conspiratorial grin. The wonder of this pond had turned the street-smart punk into a little boy hitting home runs.

"Juan! That is huge!" Cade hurried to get the net as the teen eased the large-mouth bass up to the bank. "We're going to eat good tonight."

Just as he lowered the flopping fish into the bucket of water, a movement in his peripheral vision caught his attention. Matthew jumped up and down on the bank. The tip of his cane pole bent down almost touching the water.

"Whoa, Matt!" Cade rushed over to him with the net. "I think you've got a whale."

A noise that sounded suspiciously like a snicker came from the red-headed boy's direction. Behind him, Cade paused with the net frozen in midair. He glanced across at Annalisa who sat on the bank a few feet away with Tim perched on her knee.

She nodded, the delight he was feeling reflected in her eyes.

Cade's throat clogged with emotion, but he struggled to sound normal. "Just ease him into the net, and I'll hold him up for everyone to see."

Matthew maneuvered the humongous fish into the net. He grinned while Cade held it up for inspection, but didn't make another sound.

"When am I going to catch one?" Tim asked.

Cade got Matthew's fish settled into the bucket, then walked over to where Tim was now squatting beside Annalisa. The boy waved his small pole at a dragonfly that skittered above the surface of the pond.

"It helps to keep the hook in the water, Son." Cade guided Tim's pole into the correct position.

While he held his arms around Tim, teaching him the correct way to hold the cane pole, he felt Annalisa's gaze on him. He glanced up quickly. A smile, tinged with bittersweet regret, played across her soft lips.

The smile set Cade's PI senses racing. He felt as if he'd been sucker-punched. She was leaving. He knew it as surely as if she'd told him. The sunlit day, perfect a few moments before, seemed dark and dreary.

". . .a bite! Mr. Cade!"

He jerked his attention back to Tim, who was pulling frantically on his pole. Cade scrambled to his feet, yanking the boy up with him. "Pull!"

When he was sure Tim had corralled the medium-sized bass, he eased over and grabbed the net. Cade held the flopping fish in the net. Tim squealed with joy.

"Way to go, Timbo!" Juan called.

Cade put the fish in the bucket and made a mental note to tell the teen later how proud he'd been of him in this moment.

A few weeks ago, Juan would have gloated over catching more fish. He was coming along nicely. When he went back home in the fall, hopefully his grandmother would hardly recognize her up-and-coming-juvenile-delinquent grandson.

The middle-aged woman had only had custody of Juan for a year. The social worker said she had the potential to be a good guardian to him, but first he had to lose the attitude that years of living on the streets with his drug-abusing parents had given him. That was what Cade hoped to accomplish with Juan this summer. *An attitudectomy, so to speak,* he thought, with a wry chuckle.

"What's so funny?" Annalisa's soft voice sounded beside his ear. Tim had scurried off to get another worm to re-bait his hook and, without an animated little boy between them, the overhanging trees leaning out over the bank seemed to create an intimate canopy around the couple.

Casting a glance to where Matthew and Juan stood about twenty feet or so away, he shook his head. "I'll tell you later."

Just as had happened earlier, one look at her sad expression, and he knew what she was thinking. "Unless you're thinking there might not be a later for us."

Her attempt at a laugh fell flat. "Why do you say that?"

"Are you leaving?"

"Cade." She gently touched his arm. "Let's don't talk about this right now. Not here." The pain was evident in her brown eyes. The sun glinted off the gold flecks, and he remembered the first day he'd met her. He'd thought the golden highlights in her beautiful chocolate eyes were buried treasure. Then he'd decided they were secrets that would end up causing him pain. How right he'd been.

He shook her hand off his arm and turned to the boys. "We'd better get these fish cleaned if we're going to make it to Jack Rock Hole before dark, guys."

Juan and Tim grumbled a little at having to surrender their poles, but all three boys stared with interest when Cade pulled out his pocketknife and began teaching them how to clean fish.

In spite of his earlier exasperation with her, he couldn't help but grin when Annalisa turned her back on the messy proceedings. His mother had always helped clean the fish, but his genteel grandmother had done the same as this brunette beauty and ignored the procedure.

He allowed each boy a carefully supervised turn with the knife, then took it back to filet the meat, separating it from the bones.

As he finished, he snuck a peek at Annalisa, who continued to studiously ignore them while she brushed Bubba's shoulders. "You're going to spoil that horse rotten," he called.

"I'm nice to him. He's nice to me," she retorted. "It's a give-and-take relationship."

"Well, it's time for him to give again, because we're heading out." He packed the fish in the small cooler and showed Juan where to dump the remains, explaining to the boys the difference between litter and fertilizer.

They mounted the horses and headed up the trail. Since the path was very distinct, Annalisa led the way, with the boys in the middle, and Cade bringing up the rear. Five minutes away from the pond, Tim slowed down to ride beside Cade. "How much longer?"

Cade guffawed and then laughed harder at Tim's puzzled expression.

Annalisa stopped Bubba. "What's so funny?" she called.

"I'm turning into my dad. Tim just asked me how much longer."

She grinned broadly. "Don't you imagine kids asked that

even in wagon trains?"

"I guess. I always thought it was a car thing."

"Uh. . .Mr. Cade?"

"Yeah, Timbo?"

"Does that mean you don't know how much longer?"

✦

Juan skipped another rock across the rolling water. ". . .three. . . four. . .five. Five times! That one went five times."

Annalisa grinned as Tim stealthily moved along the water's edge, obviously scoping out just the right rock. A look of pleasure crossed his face just before he bent and snatched up the stone. He slung it, but it kerplunked into the water just like the hundred other brave stones that had passed through the seven year old's hand in the last half hour.

He kicked at the rocky beach, then turned his pleading gaze back to Juan. "Show me again."

Annalisa watched the play of emotions across the teen's face. Disgust at being bothered by a baby warred with the delight of being looked up to. Delight won, and Annalisa did a mental *Yes!* as Juan patiently demonstrated again how to hold the flat stone.

She leaned back in the lawn chair. The early evening sky swirled into a panorama of reds and yellows and blues that was reminiscent of this morning's sunrise. God's power had been proven many times over in the events of today. She could see these three boys changing before her eyes.

Looking over to where Cade helped Matthew build a rock house on the shore, she couldn't be sure whose grin was broader. Matthew had smiled more today than he had in the whole time he'd been at the ranch. Now, if only he would talk.

Tears stung her eyes as she remembered what Cade had told her about Matthew. A car wreck had claimed the lives of his parents, and he'd had no relatives who'd been willing to take him. It had been impossible to place him in an adoptive home, because since the night of the accident, he hadn't spoken a word. The doctors had examined him and found no physical reason for his muteness. His counselor had chalked it up to extreme emotional trauma and concluded he would have to come back to talking on his own.

Cade had asked her to pray about it, and she would—even after she was gone. She might not be around to see the end result, but she had faith that God would allow Matthew to find the peace he needed to be able to speak again.

The thought of leaving Cade and the boys caused her chest to tighten. She sat up straight and pushed herself to her feet. Sometimes it was better not to relax.

I'm coming, Amy.

eleven

The delicious aroma of grilled fish drifted down the path to greet the firewood-toting bunch. Cade's stomach rumbled, and he picked up the pace.

"That smells wonderful!" He dumped his armload of wood in the designated campfire spot. "What are we having besides fish?"

"Corn on the cob and vegetables, all fresh off the grill. Plus some cornbread muffins I made up before we came." Annalisa's hair was pulled up in a pert ponytail cascading down her back in curls. Her freshly-scrubbed face shone like a child's.

Inexorably drawn by either the mouth-watering smell or the lovely brunette, Cade moved over to the grill area. Unfortunately, it didn't take a rocket scientist to figure out which attracted him the most. How could she look so perfect after a long hot day on the trail?

"Any chance you could spare a drink for a poor, thirsty laborer?"

With her hand on her hip, she cocked one eyebrow and waved the spatula at him. "Would it get you started on that campfire any sooner?"

"Definitely." He smiled at her mock severity.

"Well, then, I guess I'd better let you have it. We were hoping to roast marshmallows for dessert." She reached into a satchel and pulled out a collapsible juice pouch with a straw. "Hope you're not too picky. It's not exactly cold."

"Thanks. I can handle lukewarm juice." He peeled the straw off the side and unwrapped it. "But in certain things I guess I could be considered picky."

He turned and walked over to start the campfire. His family had always called him picky when it came to the opposite sex. Now that he'd met Annalisa, he realized what he'd been waiting for.

❧

The glow of the campfire illuminated four sticky, happy male faces as Annalisa shoved the last bite of marshmallow in her mouth. Cade leaned over and wiped her face with his own damp paper towel. "You must have been a Girl Scout. I'd have never thought of giving everybody a wet paper towel."

"Nope, I'm not a Girl Scout, just a very messy eater when it comes to roasted marshmallows. . .as you noticed."

"Hey! Watch this!" Tim scooped three marshmallows at once off his stick and shoved them in his mouth.

"Watch this!" Not about to be outdone by a little kid, Juan held his stick up. Five burned marshmallows sagged down from it. He held it up over his mouth and tried to eat them off before they fell to the ground. Just as he got the fourth one in his already full mouth, the last one drizzled into his black hair. "Eww! Gross!"

"Was that as sticky as Old Sweetie's kiss?" Cade drawled.

"Very funny." Juan gave his hair an ineffective swipe with his moist napkin, but Annalisa noticed, instead of getting mad, he grinned. "How am I gonna get this off me?"

"Come over here." Cade stood up and walked over to the bucket, which Annalisa had put some clean river water in for washing. "Bend over." He filled the long-handled ladle and poured the water over Juan's head. Juan came up swinging water from his hair like a dog. Everyone except Matthew laughed, and Annalisa thought she might have heard a chuckle from him.

"Whoa, Buddy." Cade offered the bar soap. Juan snatched it from his hand and lathered up his hair. "We'll be done in a minute." As soon as Juan had a good lather, Cade poured clean water to rinse, then handed him a towel.

"Juan's playing beauty shop," Tim called, pointing and laughing.

"Oh, yeah?" Juan's eyes sparked anger for a second, then he smiled. "At least I don't have no sticky hair anymore. Thanks, Mr. Cade."

"No problem." He slung his arm across Juan's shoulder, and they walked back over to the campfire.

Cade's patience with these boys astonished Annalisa. Her own father would have probably smacked her for getting marshmallow in her hair. Or at least made her wear the gooey mess the rest of the night.

"Let's all get washed up and ready for bed, then I want us to talk about something." Cade herded the boys over to the wash bucket, then poured them each some drinking water in a cup to brush their teeth with.

When they'd gathered around the fire again, Cade stood up. "We're going to do a little experiment."

The firelight revealed the curiosity in all three boys' eyes.

"First, I need a volunteer."

Three hands shot up in the air.

"Juan, come on up here."

Juan tossed a victorious smile to the younger boys and sauntered up to where Cade stood.

"Turn around and face them." Juan turned around toward Annalisa and the other boys.

Cade stood about two feet behind him. "Fall straight back."

"What?" Juan swung around to face Cade.

"Come on now, you volunteered." He pivoted Juan forward. "Look straight ahead and fall backward."

Juan turned around, and Annalisa almost laughed at the look of concentration on his face. "Aw, man. I can't."

"Sure you can. You know I'll catch you, don't you?"

"Yeah, I guess, but. . ."

"I'll catch you. Now, fall."

"Okay, here goes nuthin'." Juan suddenly looked younger than his thirteen years. He squeezed his eyes shut and fell backward into Cade's arms.

Cade caught him gently and then lifted him back to standing. Relief radiated from Juan's face. "That was sort of fun." Cade held up his hand, and Juan gave him a big high-five.

"I'm glad. Now go sit down before your legs give way."

"My legs hold me up just fine. I ain't no scaredy-cat." As Juan strolled back to his chair, careful to maintain his cool, Cade winked at Annalisa. She put her hand over her mouth to cover her grin.

"Matthew, you want to give it a try?"

Matthew nodded and jumped from his chair and ran up to Cade. Before the man said anything, Matthew turned around and faced the boys and Annalisa, standing a couple of feet in front of Cade.

Cade squared himself with his eager volunteer and held out his arms. "Okay, Matthew, fall straight back."

The red-haired boy didn't hesitate like Juan had done. Cade caught him easily and set him back upright. Matthew's grin split his freckled face, and he energetically returned Cade's high-five and scurried back to his chair.

Before Matthew was in his seat, Tim was standing in front of Cade, immediately falling back in his arms. Cade scooped him up and swung him around while his shrieks of delight echoed through the hills. Out of breath and laughing, Cade put the child down and gently pointed him to his chair.

When everyone was seated again, Cade's smiling face grew solemn. "Juan?"

"Yeah?"

"Why did you trust me to catch you?"

" 'Cause you said you would?"

"Yes, but, hasn't anyone ever told you they'd do something and then not done it?"

Juan dropped his head. "Sure have."

"So did you trust them next time?"

"Nah." He half-mumbled the answer.

"Then why did you know I'd catch you?"

Juan looked up and his black eyes glittered in the firelight. " 'Cause you ain't never let us down yet."

Annalisa could see Cade fighting to suppress the urge to correct Juan's English, but she applauded his restraint. This wasn't the time for grammar lessons.

"I hope I haven't. So, in other words, we wouldn't fall back with someone behind us if we didn't know they'd catch us, would we?"

Matthew shook his head vigorously.

"Uh-uh," Tim said.

"No way!" Juan chimed in.

"What about if somebody you don't know, or do know but don't trust. . ." Cade said each word deliberately, and Annalisa knew he was willing the boys to let the message sink in. ". . .tries to get you to do something dangerous, like take drugs or ride in a hot car?"

"I wouldn't," Tim piped up, and Annalisa suppressed a smile at his earnestness.

"Me either." Juan's voice wasn't perky like Tim's, but he sounded like he was firm on the subject.

Matthew shook his head.

"Boys, you make me proud. You're some of the smartest boys I know." Cade sank back down in his lawn chair. "I've got one more question for you, though. What if I was standing behind you about to catch you and a snake bit my leg or a panther jumped on my back?" Tim gasped, and Annalisa appreciated Cade's quick change. "Or a squirrel fell out of the tree and landed right on my head?"

Tim giggled.

"I imagine you'd drop us," Juan offered.

"I imagine I might very well do that, Juan. It wouldn't be my fault, but the ground would be just as hard and hurt just as bad. Wouldn't it?"

"Uh-huh." All three boys nodded.

"So even if a person is someone you can trust, you can't trust them completely, can you?" They shook their heads. "Why not?"

"Because a squirrel might fall on their head." Tim extended his fingers and squeezed the top of his head, crossing his eyes.

After the laughter died down, Cade nodded. "That's right. Something out of their control could make them not trustworthy, because they're human. I want to share with you guys one of my favorite Bible verses. It tells us there's someone we can always trust in. . . Someone we can depend on even more than we do ourselves."

"God!" Tim called out.

Cade smiled at the boy. "Yep, that's right, Timbo. I'm glad to see George's Bible lessons are paying off. This particular lesson comes from the book of Proverbs, chapter three, verses five and six. This is what it says, 'Trust in the Lord with all thine heart; and lean not unto thine own understanding. In all thy ways acknowledge him, and he shall direct thy paths.' "

Annalisa felt her throat clog with emotion. Had she been allowing God to direct her path? Surely it was His will that she find her sister, wasn't it?

"In other words, if you trust God and count on Him and let it be known that's what you're doing, He'll show you how to go."

"What if a squirrel falls on his head?"

"Don't be silly!" Juan shook his head. "Nothing can hurt God or keep Him from being there to catch you."

"Not even a wildcat?"

Juan shook his head. "Not even a snake."

Tears filled Annalisa's eyes, and when she met Cade's gaze, even in the firelight, she could tell his were moist, as well.

No one spoke for a minute, then Cade cleared his throat. "Jesus loves me, this I know. . ."

The boys and Annalisa joined in, and the chorus of the old familiar song rang out through the dark night. Annalisa's heart was so full it felt like it would burst.

"Let's pray." They all bowed and, for a second, all that could be heard were the crickets chirping. "Father, Thank You for this day. We've had so much fun, and we know that without You, none of this would have happened. Lord, please be with each of these boys—Juan, Matthew, and Tim. Help them to grow up strong and brave in Your service, trusting always in You, and allowing You to direct their paths. Please be with Annalisa and help her find the peace she seeks. And be with me, Lord, in everything I do. In Jesus' name, amen."

Even the boys seemed subdued, but content, as they all quietly put the fire out and used the lantern to light their way while they got settled in the tents.

Once everyone was in bed and a whole string of good

nights had been said, Annalisa contemplated the many sides of Cade McFadden until she finally drifted off to sleep.

❧

Annalisa opened her eyes. The shadowy material above her face looked unfamiliar, but the cry that had jarred her from a sound sleep was very real. She sat up, desperately trying to get her bearings. Cade's camping trip—she was in a tent. She glanced at Tim, who lay in his sleeping bag next to her. The seven-year-old hadn't protested when he'd been assigned to her tent. She'd been afraid he'd think it was babyish, especially since the other two boys were sleeping in the tent with Cade. Had the embarrassment caused Tim to have a bad dream?

His long lashes swept across his cheeks, and her heart contracted at the thought of him having nightmares. But his even breathing seemed to show no evidence of distress. She sat, listening to the crickets, with the sleeping bag bunched around her waist. She'd brought a lightweight jogging suit to sleep in, and she'd been warm when they'd first gone to bed, but now a cool breeze was blowing through the screen door.

Another yell broke through her thoughts. She took one more look at Tim, who still appeared to be sleeping soundly, then jumped up and unzipped the door. She slipped her feet into her beach sandals and hurried the few inches to Cade's tent. He'd laughed at her for insisting they be so close but, unused to sleeping outside, she hadn't cared.

"Cade? Are the boys okay?" She whispered, just in case anyone was a sound sleeper and hadn't awakened in all the commotion.

Silence.

"Cade!" Horrible visions of a wild beast breaking into the tent ran through her mind, then she put her hand over her mouth as she realized he would have had to zip the door back behind him after pulling out the three campers.

"NO! Stop! Don't run!" Cade yelled the words from inside the tent.

Annalisa jumped back from the door. As the loud commands faded into the night, nothing but the crickets sounded in the inky darkness. "Cade?" She didn't bother with a whisper.

"Annalisa?" Cade's groggy voice didn't resemble the panicked tones of a moment before.

"Are you okay?"

"Yeah." A long pause followed. "I guess. Are you?"

"Yeah. You feel like talking for a few minutes?" She hated to just ask him about the dreams, but she knew from personal experience that if he went back to sleep right now the dream was likely to pick back up where it had left off.

"Sure, if you want to."

"Are Juan and Matthew still asleep?"

"Yeah."

She heard a rustling sound and then the zipper of the tent door. In spite of the situation, she couldn't help but smile at his dark hair standing on end. Her grin abruptly faded when she realized she must look at least as rumpled. She was thankful for the semi-darkness.

He took her elbow and guided her to the lawn chairs they'd set up earlier along the small bluff overlooking the river. She sank down into her chair and shivered.

"Here." His voice, still husky from sleep, echoed across the river. He handed her a lap quilt.

"Thanks for thinking of that. Now who's the Girl Scout? Oops, I mean Boy Scout." She smiled and wrapped the blanket around her shoulders.

They sat in silence looking at the moonlight dappling the water.

"Annalisa. . .what woke you up?"

She stared at him. The silver light reflecting in his eyes made them inscrutable. "Why?"

"You know, don't you?" He turned his head and stared at the water. The moments ticked by, but she didn't know what to say. Finally he spoke again. "You heard me having a nightmare."

"I thought it was one of the boys."

"But when you figured out it was me, you wanted me to get up and come out here so it wouldn't start again."

"Yes." She reached over and slid her hand into his. "I thought you could use a friend."

"Thanks." He squeezed her hand then turned it over, making little circles on her palm with his thumb. "You were right."

"Want to talk about the dream?"

He cleared his throat. "It's always different, but always the same. A child, usually a boy, is in some kind of terrible danger, and it's up to me to save him."

"Do you?"

He rubbed his hand down his face and didn't speak for several seconds. "No."

"Have you been having these dreams ever since Joey's dad killed himself?"

"Yes, off and on. When I first moved to the ranch, they stopped, but then. . ."

"Then I came?"

"I'm not sure that's why they started back."

"I wanted you to find Amy, and you felt like your absolution was over. So the dreams started again." His angry reaction the night she'd asked him to help her made more sense. "I'm sorry, Cade. I understand now why you can't help me. I won't ask you again."

Even as she said the words, the end of the road rushed up to meet her. She couldn't stay at the Circle-M, seeking her own happiness, anymore. Tears filled her eyes at the thought.

He stood and pulled her to her feet. Fireflies flitted through the night sky and intermingled with the innumerable stars that decorated the canopy of heaven. When he gathered her in his arms, she relaxed against him and hid her face in his shirt.

"Hey, now. If I wanted my shirt wet, I'd have jumped in the river." His soft voice sent shivers down her spine.

She leaned back and met his gaze. "Sorry."

"You know I was kidding you." He caressed her cheek with his thumb. "I'd take your tears over river water any day." She started to speak, and he shook his head. "Wait. That didn't come out exactly like I meant it."

"Oh, really? I thought you were saying you'd rather make me cry than go on a fun float trip."

"Actually I'd rather make you laugh tonight and take you on a fun float trip tomorrow. How about it?"

"Sounds like a deal I can't refuse."

"I know just how to seal the bargain." His thumb moved to her lower lip.

"What?" She looked at him to see what he was talking about, then shivered again as his mouth lowered to hers. Cade's kiss was everything Annalisa had come to expect of him—strong and sweet. She'd never felt so safe, yet there was nothing brotherly about this embrace. Love washed over her in great rushing waves.

He pulled back, and they stared at each other as the river babbled beside them. With a poignant smile, he released her. "Get some sleep. We both need to get some rest if we're going to corral those boys on the river tomorrow."

"Good night, Cade."

They walked a little distance apart from each other back to

the tents. When they reached the doors, he spoke one more time in a whisper. "Annalisa. . ."

"Yeah?"

"Thanks for waking me up."

She couldn't speak around the lump in her throat, so she nodded and groped for the door zipper through a fresh blur of tears.

He reached over and unzipped it for her, then quickly unfastened his own door and went inside.

She nestled back into her sleeping bag and tried to ignore her trembling arms and legs. She prayed for a long time, then, mindful of the other campers so close, shed silent tears until sleep finally overtook her.

twelve

Cade had gotten up before good daylight to take the horses to the pen a few miles down river. The trip there had been quick, riding Duke and leading the others, but the journey back had taken longer than he expected. He probably should have left Annalisa and the boys a note.

Too late to worry about that now, he thought, as he approached the camp. The smell of bacon and eggs frying made his mouth water. Annalisa had her back to him and once again, he was struck by her graceful movements. From the silence, he surmised the three boys were still asleep. She probably hadn't even realized he was gone.

His mischievous streak kicked into overdrive, and he tiptoed to his tent. He squatted down facing her and fastened the zipper loudly. She spun around to look at him, and he stood up and stretched.

"Good morning." He covered his mouth as if to yawn.

"Good morning, Sleepyhead. I've never known you to sleep so late."

"This fresh air does strange things to a person," Cade said.

"I guess."

"Hey!" Cade strove for a surprised tone. "Where are the horses?"

Annalisa looked up from the skillet. "Oh. I don't know. Maybe they got tired of hanging around." She bent over to dig in the satchel bag for something.

"Annalisa!" Cade couldn't keep the exasperation from his

voice. "Did you understand? I said the horses are gone."

"Yeah, I heard you." She barely glanced up from buttering bread.

He was stunned by her reaction, or lack thereof, to be more specific. Somehow he'd expected much, much more. "Don't you care about the horses?"

"Sure I do. As a matter of fact, why don't you go look for them? I'll save you some breakfast."

"Aargh. . ." He sat down in the lawn chair and shook his head. "I can't believe you. I thought you'd be worried."

"Worried?" She looked up and winked. "When I saw you on Duke leading the others away before dawn? What's to worry about?"

He sprang to his feet. "In all these years, my brothers have never gotten the best of me when I played a joke on them. But it didn't take you five minutes to have me ready to pull my hair out."

She threw back her long mane of hair and laughed. "I'm sorry for disappointing you."

Cade knew he should have been disappointed, but he was secretly delighted that she'd turned the tables on him. "That's okay. It had to happen sometime. Better you than Clint or Jake or especially Holt."

"I didn't do anything special, Cade. I just happened to be in the right place at the right time."

"I'm starting to think that's the secret of happiness." He realized again how thankful he was that she'd come along to his place at this particular time in his life.

Annalisa laid the food out on plates. "So, did you take the horses somewhere just to play an elaborate prank or is there a method to your madness?"

Cade glanced heavenward in mock despair. "Now, she's

interested." They laughed together. "Actually, I had a reason. . . I was trying to make it easy on us. When we inflate the rafts and put all of our stuff in them, we can float down the river a few miles and the horses will be waiting for us in a pen at the end of the line."

"There's an ingenious idea. I guess I hadn't really thought about what we'd do after we got downstream."

"Good thing one of us thinks ahead," he said.

She snorted. "Where would we be without you, Cade McFadden?"

"Is Mr. Cade going somewhere?" Tim's voice sounded sleepy and a little fearful.

"No!" Cade held out his arms and the boy ran into his embrace. "Lord willing, I'm here to stay." As he wrapped his arms around the child, he prayed that he could be a permanent fixture in Tim's life. When he glanced up again at the smiling brunette, he couldn't help but attach an addendum to the prayer.

He stood up and clasped Tim's hand. "Let's go wake up Juan and Matthew." As they approached the tents, Cade held his finger to his lips. "Shh. . ." He squatted beside the tent and made a whistle sound. "Bob-white! Bob-white!"

Tim bit back a giggle.

"Somebody turn the volume down!" Juan's groggy voice drifted out of the tent.

Cade, Tim, and Annalisa laughed so loudly that Juan unzipped the door, and, along with Matthew, stuck his head out.

"I guess we know who will be the last ones in the river," Cade said.

Juan grabbed Matthew's arm and pulled him back, then quickly zipped the tent door. Less than three minutes later, both boys emerged, fully clothed and grinning.

The boys made a much better audience than Annalisa had for Cade's missing horses gag, but before they could get upset, he reassured them. After eating a hasty breakfast, the campers broke camp and piled all the camping gear in a neat pile for George to retrieve later. They applied sunblock and aired up the small rubber rafts. Everyone but Tim had his or her own boat.

Social Services had assured him that all three boys were proficient swimmers, and he knew their life jackets were fastened tightly, but he still felt more comfortable keeping the youngest with him. His heart swelled when, instead of grumbling at the arrangements, Tim pumped his fist in the air with a big "Yahoo!"

Cade headed over to where Annalisa stood at the edge of the water. In a motion becoming familiar to him, she swooped up her mass of curls and swirled them into a twist, securing it with a big clippie thing. She then gave considerable attention to the fasteners on her life jacket.

"You nervous?"

She looked up. "Who me?"

"Uh-oh. I knew I should have asked other questions besides, 'Do you swim?' Is your swimming experience comparable to your horseback-riding experience?"

"Not hardly," she said, with a chuckle. "I really can swim. I'm even certified to rescue someone if need be."

"Then why are you triple-checking your life jacket fasteners?"

She offered a rueful grin. "I've never swum except in a pool. I'm a little apprehensive about rafting."

"This is nothing like you see on television. We'll be lucky if we see any white water at all. Holes of water where the speed of the water moderately increases are about all the rapids we get on Fourche River."

She looked thoughtfully out over the gently rolling water. "Let's just call them not-quite-so-slows instead of rapids, okay? I think that would make me feel better."

He laughed. "For you, Annalisa Davis—anything."

❧

The nose of the navy blue and red rubber raft dipped down in the water and scooped up a spray of cold liquid onto Annalisa. "Whoa!" Her stomach had dipped as well, but the sensation wasn't entirely unpleasant, especially considering she'd managed to stay upright through the small rapid.

"Uh, Annalisa," Cade called from his nearby raft. " 'Whoa' only works with horses."

"Now you tell me. Why didn't you add that in with your little speech about technical things like going toward the open vees of water and avoiding the points of closed vees?"

"I guess it slipped my mind."

She grinned at the picture he and Tim made—working together to keep the little boat moving. Juan and Matthew were in their own rafts on either side of Cade. She was bringing up the rear.

They'd come through three little areas of white water, but following Cade's simple direction, no one had been in the water. From the way Juan continued to rock his boat, though, Annalisa figured the teen was ready to get wet.

Since she'd cleared the rapids, they set off again at a leisurely pace, floating through a wide, deep hole of water. The boys paddled, but Cade wouldn't allow them to get too far ahead. They'd advance a little, then turn and paddle back upstream to reach the others.

Annalisa leaned back against the cushioned pillow of her raft. Gigantic leafy trees lined the banks of the river. Their limbs almost interlocked in a canopy over the water, leaving only a small space of blue sky peeking out of the green foliage. She closed her eyes and soaked up the peace. Crickets sang up and down the banks, and the only other sound was the lapping of the water at the side of her boat and the occasional swish of Juan or Matthew's paddles in the water.

Drip, drip, drip. Frowning, she opened one eye. It was supposed to be sunny all day. The sky looked blue with only an occasional white cloud drifting by. But she had felt a light sprinkle. She glanced at Cade and Tim. They had their backs to her, seeming to be fascinated by a leaf floating in the water. Juan and Matthew were paddling over to take a look.

She closed her eyes again. Drip, drip, drip. She decided to ignore it. Suddenly, a huge splash of water landed in her face. She opened both eyes and jumped up to sitting. All the boys had their backs turned, but Cade's shoulders were shaking.

"Cade McFadden!" Her yell rang out through the bluffs.

He turned around, the picture of innocence, other than the grin that tugged at the corner of his handsomely chiseled mouth. "Yes?"

"Something about this river turns you into a kid, doesn't it?"

His grin burst forth, unrestrained. "Yes, Ma'am, I suppose it does. You think we've discovered the fountain of youth?"

Juan laughed and Tim joined in.

"I sincerely doubt it." In spite of her wet face and hair, she couldn't stay mad at him when he looked so boyish and relaxed. He'd carried the world on his shoulders far too long. "Why? Were you thinking I needed a double dose of the fountain of youth? Particularly on my face?"

"Now, Annalisa, you know better than that. You already look like a teenager."

"Are we almost back to the horses? Now this water's not only affecting your actions but your eyesight, as well."

"I beg to differ, but as a matter of fact, we have one more section of rapids up ahead, then we'll be at the pen where the horses are."

Juan and Tim groaned, and Matthew looked crestfallen.

"Aren't you boys getting hungry?" Cade asked.

"No!"

"Huh-uh."

"Tell you what," Annalisa offered, "when we get to the horses, could the boys swim a bit while I fix the sandwiches?"

"Yeah!"

"YIPPEE!"

Cade grinned at her. "I suppose that wouldn't hurt anything."

The last rapid was upon them, and Cade and Tim prepared to lead the way. "Juan," Cade called to the teen, who was still rocking his boat from side to side. "Let's try to stay dry until we get to the swimming hole."

Annalisa expected Juan to argue, but he neatly swooshed his raft through the white water and waited calmly beside Cade and Tim for her and Matthew. He'd definitely come a long way.

They all pulled their boats up to the shore, and the boys leaped out into the water. Annalisa was determined not to get wet, since she'd made it this far. She eased to standing. Cade reached out a hand to help her, but she didn't step quite high enough to clear the tubed edge of the raft. Instead of leaping gracefully onto the beach, she tumbled into Cade's arms.

"Look!" Tim's high voice echoed across the water. "Annalisa trusts Mr. Cade."

Cade, his face mere inches from hers and his arms around her tightly, raised one eyebrow. "Is that true?"

She felt heat creep up her cheeks. "Yes, I suppose it is."

"I'm glad." He gave her one quick squeeze and released her.

Heart thudding, she hurried up to the horses, with the others trailing behind her. The animals were glad to see them. Bubba, in particular, whinnied at Annalisa as she fixed the sandwiches. She was going to miss him when she went.

And he was the least of her heartaches. Suddenly, she realized Cade wasn't the only one who'd let the river take his troubles for awhile. She hadn't given one thought to leaving Circle-M while they were floating. Now that her feet were back on solid ground, and they were about to head back to the ranch, it was time to face the inevitable again.

thirteen

The five horseback riders topped the final hill. The Circle-M homestead sprawled in front of them. In unspoken agreement, they paused, gazing down at the intricate arrangement of buildings that dotted the rugged landscape. Cade twisted in his saddle to examine the expressions of his traveling companions.

Tim was an open book. Excitement and happiness coated his face as surely as the sunblock he'd lathered on that morning. Matthew smiled, but a sliver of sadness hovered, threatening to overcome the grin. Juan stared at the ranch, and Cade easily recognized the emotion that played across his dark countenance. Peace. The teen was finally seeing the value of living above the war zone.

As the others continued to drink in the scenery, Cade's gaze rested on Annalisa's face. A poignant half-smile touched her lips, but her big chocolate eyes brimmed with tears. She turned and met his gaze for an agonizing second.

She looked away and flicked Bubba gently with the reins. "C'mon, Bubba. Giddy up."

The boys followed. Cade brought up the rear, wishing each clip-clop of the horses' hooves could be taking them backward in time, instead of on toward a future that undoubtedly held painful good-byes.

❧

"Mr. George! You can walk!" Tim leaped off his horse and ran across the barn lot to where George and Marta stood waiting.

Annalisa smiled as Marta deftly intercepted the youngster.

She scooped him up, then leaned him over to hug George, who was resting pretty heavily against the fence.

The others dismounted and hurried over to the couple.

"Hey! How's that ankle?" Cade asked.

"The doctor said it was too far from my heart to kill me."

Marta cast an exasperated glance heavenward. "Your corny jokes may kill me before we get you back on your feet. I think you sit around and think those up just to get at me." Her grin took the sting out of her words.

"You know you love them, so don't pretend you don't." George reached over and took her hand.

Marta blushed. "Well, anyway," she said, turning her attention back to Cade and Annalisa, "it's sprained, not broken, thank the Lord!"

Annalisa smiled at her friend's obvious attraction for her husband of twenty-five years. Would she and Cade still feel that kind of electricity after so long?

Shock coursed through her. When had she started thinking in terms of the distant future with Cade? She'd thought she was guarding her heart, but apparently she'd been wrong. She smiled at Marta and mumbled something appropriate, excusing herself to groom Bubba.

Until after Sunday lunch the next day, Annalisa performed her duties without allowing herself to be drawn into conversations or become involved in the lives of the other Circle-M residents. She sat by herself at church, slipping in at the last minute, so she wouldn't be noticed.

Now, she stood at the sink, scrubbing the pots and pans, and reflected on how colorless her life had been for the last twenty-four hours. Funny how she'd thought she could reduce the pain of what she was going to have to tell Cade. Instead she just regretted not making the most of every second here.

"You feeling okay?" The concern in Cade's voice was evident.

"I guess." She turned around and dried her hands on a towel.

He perched on a barstool. "Want to talk about it?"

"Not really." She shook her head with a rueful grin, but slid into the seat beside him. "Oh, Cade. This is harder than at the first when I was trying to tell you about Amy."

He reached over and took her hand.

"The thing is. . ." She smiled as he squeezed her hand.

Just as she opened her mouth to tell him she was giving her two-week notice, Juan came running in. "Hurry! It's Tim. He's bad."

Annalisa glanced at Cade. "Not again!"

They ran for the bunkhouse without speaking.

Marta looked up from the boy as they entered. "We used the inhaler, but it doesn't seem to be helping this time." Her voice was calm, but her eyes conveyed a message of urgency to the adults.

Cade scooped Tim into his arms and headed toward his vehicle. "You and I will just take a ride into town, Tim. I've been meaning to introduce you to the local doctors, anyway." He looked at Marta. "Will you call the ER and let them know we're coming?" He glanced at the boy's blue face. "On second thought, call 911, too, and have an ambulance meet us. I'll have my hazard lights on. If they leave now, we should meet at the old Stokes' store."

"Cade, may I ride with you? I can sit by Tim and keep him company." Her voice shook, and his gaze met hers. She breathed a sigh of relief when he nodded.

He carefully deposited the boy into the backseat of the sports-utility vehicle and fastened the seat belt across him.

Annalisa stood back as Cade ruffled his hair. "Hang in there, Buddy." His voice sounded cheerful, but when he turned around, she saw deep lines of worry etched in his face.

"Pray," he said softly.

Annalisa nodded, then slid in beside Tim. She reached over to take his little hand in hers. His hand was sweaty, and his face was still blue. His breathing didn't seem any better either as Cade pulled down the bumpy driveway.

Annalisa began to sing a lullaby she'd sung to Amy daily the first year of the child's life. She smoothed Tim's hair in time with the gentle melody. He relaxed against her, and his breathing, though still labored, became more even.

She met Cade's gaze in the rearview mirror. Terror leaped at her from his eyes, and she stumbled over the words to the song. She nodded to him and pointed upward, hoping he would process the reassurance that God was in control.

He turned his attention back to his driving as he pulled off the gravel onto the highway. Annalisa stared out the window as the scenery whizzed by, whole forests seeming to blend to a tiny clump of trees with Cade's speed. She wondered at the fact that no policeman stopped them as the Maynard city limits sign came and went, the small town seeming to appear and disappear in the blink of an eye.

Just as she completed the song, Tim's wheezing accelerated.

"Should we try the inhaler again?" she asked Cade.

"Yes. No, wait. I hear the ambulance coming." He glanced over his shoulder at Tim. "Hang in there, Bud."

"I'm scared." Tim barely got the words out between wheezes.

Dear God, please keep him safe, Annalisa prayed silently. She could see Cade's lips moving and realized he was doing the same.

"I'm going with you, Tim," Cade reassured the boy, then met her gaze again in the rearview mirror. "Can you drive and follow the ambulance to the hospital? I need to go with him."

The helplessness she saw reflected in his face reminded her of her own swirling emotions the day she'd lost Amy. She nodded, then realized he'd already shifted his attention to finding a place to pull off for the ambulance that was barreling toward them. "Sure."

❧

Cade jumped out and retrieved Tim from the backseat. He cradled the boy in his arms and ran toward the ambulance.

A huge bald man, sporting a goatee and one gold earring, reached for the boy. "Here, Sir. I'll take him from here."

Cade grasped Tim, stunned by the feeling that if he could keep holding the child, he could somehow keep him safe. Shaking off the crazy thought, he surrendered Tim to the EMT. When he hurried alongside the man to the ambulance, the attendant glanced at him. "We'll meet you at the hospital."

"No! I'm going with him. I promised."

"Sir." The other EMT, a smallish woman with graying hair cropped short in a no-nonsense style, grasped Cade's arm. Her blue eyes shone with sympathy as her partner loaded Tim in the ambulance. "You can go, but there's not a lot of room to move around in there. The boy would be better served by you letting us do our job."

For one of the few times in his life, Cade felt uncertain about what to do. He instinctively glanced at Annalisa, who stood a little to the side of the ambulance. She nodded, and he knew she was right. "Okay. What's your name?"

The gray-haired woman smiled. "I'm Nancy. We'll take care of him as if he were our own." She hurried to jump in the back with Tim.

"Tim!" Cade craned his head to catch the boy's weak gaze. The sight of his blue face clogged Cade's throat, but he forced a smile. "This is Nancy. She's going to help you breathe. We'll be right behind the ambulance in the car. Hang in there, Buddy. I'll see you in a few minutes."

Nancy closed the door on his last word, and the other EMT slid in the driver's seat.

Cade watched the red lights flashing as the emergency vehicle quickly drove out of sight. He felt Annalisa squeeze his shoulder, and he put his own hand over hers for a second. Then, without a word, they hurried to the SUV and climbed in. He threw the four-wheel-drive into gear and maneuvered down the curvy highway at a speed best reserved for the interstate.

After a few minutes of silence, Annalisa spoke. "Are you okay?"

Cade followed her glance to his white knuckles on the steering wheel. "I don't know. . . I knew it was for his own good, but I couldn't bear to give him up. What if I lose him?"

"He's in good hands." Her voice was soft, but the confidence in her tone made him feel better.

"I know. I have no doubt they're adequately trained at what they do. Certainly more so than I am."

"I'm sure they are, but theirs weren't the hands I meant. I was talking about God's hands. Tim's in God's hands."

He nodded. "You're right."

They rode in silence, until he pulled into the ER entrance. The EMTs were rolling Tim through the automatic doors. "Will you park?"

"Sure. I'll be right in. Just remember, I'm praying."

He nodded his thanks and in a few long strides covered the distance to the ER doors.

The receptionist nodded. "They're working on him now.

Thankfully, Louise from Social Services here in town was able to come by and sign for him to receive care. She arrived a few minutes before the ambulance. The doctor will be out to talk to you in a few minutes."

"Is he. . . ?" Cade's worst fears clogged his throat.

"He's being well taken care of. You need to fill out these forms." The woman made a small gesture toward a clipboard, then apparently recognizing the despair in Cade's soul, she relented. "I'm sure he's going to be fine. By the time you get the forms completed, you should be able to see him."

Cade filled out the blanks numbly, praying that he was answering correctly. When a soft hand touched his shoulder, he swung around to meet Annalisa's concerned gaze.

"How is he?"

He shook his head. "I don't know. They said they'd come and get me."

"Oh, Cade. I know waiting can be so hard."

Cade handed the clipboard to the harried-looking woman behind the window.

"Thank you, Mr. McFadden. If you're ready, I'll take you back to Tim."

Annalisa hung back, and Cade could see the uncertainty on her face. With a nod, he put his hand to the small of her back and escorted her down the hallway. Although he'd included her partly because she cared so much about Tim, he knew his motives weren't totally altruistic. Selfishly, he wanted her there because it was becoming natural to face life's daily difficulties with her by his side.

fourteen

As they entered Tim's room, Cade felt Annalisa slip her hand into his and give it a squeeze. When he saw the slight figure lying so pale on the gurney, he gripped her hand tighter and looked expectantly at the woman in a white jacket who turned to face him.

"Mr. McFadden?"

"Yes."

"I'm Dr. Johannsen." Annalisa quickly relaxed her grip so he could shake the doctor's extended hand.

"How is he?"

"Much better. He had a violent asthmatic attack. Your quick thinking helped save him. . ."

"Thank you, God," Annalisa murmured.

Cade nodded in agreement.

They moved closer to the bed. Cade couldn't take his eyes off Tim. He was alive, and he was on his way back to normal.

Dr. Johannsen cleared her throat. Cade looked up to meet her gaze. Her weather-lined face was kind, but he could see she was struggling for the words to tell him something he might not like. "It's likely that an allergen of some sort set this off." Her eyes shone with sympathy. "It's even more likely, given the fact that you live on a ranch, that the allergen is hay or something similar."

"Hay?" Cade frowned. "Tim's lived at the ranch for a month and has only had one small attack. He's around hay every day. Besides, he wasn't around hay before he came to us."

"Asthma remains somewhat of a mystery. I know you mean well, Mr. McFadden, but my first responsibility is to Tim." Her voice took on a defensive tone that Cade knew didn't bode well. "With this in mind, I spoke to Louise from our local Social Services. I'm sorry, but she recommended that I call Janet Melton of the Pulaski County Department of Health and Human Services, who is the supervisor in charge of Tim's care."

Cade cringed. Ms. Melton was his contact's supervisor, and she'd been doubtful of his ranch idea from the beginning. "I see." He looked over at Tim, who still lay unmoving in the bed. "Will he be able to go home tonight?"

"After we were sure the attack was over, we gave him something to help him rest. We'd like to keep him a few more hours for observation, then you may take him back to the ranch. I strongly recommend you keep a close eye on him, though."

Struggling not to feel offended by the doctor's attitude, Cade assured her they would. She exited the room shortly after, leaving him and Annalisa alone with Tim.

Cade approached the bed with a grateful heart. He looked up to see tears of thankfulness in Annalisa's eyes. "Will you pray with me?"

She nodded.

He cleared his throat and spoke softly. "Dear Father, thank You so much for making Tim better. Please give me wisdom concerning his health and help me to do the best for him. . .no matter what I personally want. In Jesus' name, amen."

After the prayer, they sank down into the vinyl chairs beside the bed and sat in silence for a few minutes.

Suddenly Annalisa spoke. "Today when you were giving Tim to the EMT. . ." Her eyes had a faraway look and her voice dropped so low, he leaned forward to hear. "It was so much like when I had to turn Amy over to the social worker, it was eerie."

Cade remembered how he'd known deep down Tim would be better going with the ambulance attendant. Had Annalisa felt that about Amy, as well? Her tenacious search for the girl certainly didn't indicate that. "It was hard, but I knew it would be the best for Tim. It would have made no sense for me to hold onto him. I'm not a paramedic."

She either missed or chose to ignore his reference, but continued like he hadn't spoken. "After I ran away to Georgia, I got a job as a waitress in a small roadside café. One of the girls I waitressed with took me home with her my second night in town. From that moment on, her mother claimed me. They were Christians, and it didn't take very long living with them for me to want for myself the peace they had."

"That's wonderful." Cade silently thanked God for finding the homeless girl a Christian home.

"About a month after I became a Christian, I was studying the Bible when I came across a verse. Isaiah 40:31. 'But they that wait upon the Lord shall renew their strength; they shall mount up with wings as eagles; they shall run, and not be weary; and they shall walk, and not faint.' "

Her deep brown eyes met his. "I knew then. I knew that if I waited. . . If I waited, God would give me Amy back."

Even though he didn't like where this was going, Cade couldn't tear his gaze from hers.

"From that night on, that verse was my constant companion. When I was tired and despairing of ever being able to save enough money to find Amy and make a home for her, I'd repeat it. When the other girls would date and get married, I'd repeat it. It's gotten me through my whole adult life." She broke the gaze and looked at her hands, then back up at him. "Until now."

"I don't understand." Cade shook his head. "You don't believe that anymore?" Could it be that she did finally see that Amy was better off with the family she knew?

"I still believe it. But since I've come to the ranch, it's almost like that is what I've been waiting for all these years. The beauty of the land, the boys. . .you." Her voice faded so low on the last word, he wasn't sure she'd really said it. "I feel like I'm betraying my mother. Like I'm forgetting Amy."

"You'll never forget Amy. But you can ask God to help you let her go." Cade knew he'd gone too far when Annalisa's normally open face shut down like someone had pulled down the blinds.

"No!" She jumped up. "I'm going to get some coffee. Do you want some?"

"Sure."

❧

When Annalisa re-entered Tim's room a half-hour later with two cups of coffee, she was grateful Cade didn't bring up the subject of Amy again. Instead he set out to be charming, keeping her covering her mouth to smother laughter as he filled her in on some of the recent antics of the boys.

They kept their voices low, and Tim didn't stir, but in his sleep his face took on a more normal color that relieved both adults and made the nurse happy too.

"Do you think Matthew will ever talk?" Cade asked.

"I think so. I really got my hopes up when he laughed on the trip. Didn't you?"

He nodded. "I'm not giving up. He's growing closer to the horses every day. I thought sure I saw his mouth moving close to Old Sweetie's ear, so maybe he's talking to someone."

"What can we do?" Annalisa asked, almost rhetorically.

"Wait," Cade answered, but as soon as he'd said it he cleared his throat as if realizing he'd brought up a taboo subject. "George and Marta sure are doing a good job, aren't they? Marta's worked so hard to make the bunkhouse a home for the boys."

Annalisa and Cade managed to chat away the next few hours without either one bringing up Amy or waiting.

Tim awakened and after he ate a hearty hospital supper and drank some juice, Dr. Johannsen released him.

Just as they were leaving the cubicle, a nurse called to Cade. "Mr. McFadden, you have a phone call on line one." Since Cade had already called George and Marta, he and Annalisa exchanged a puzzled look.

"I'll take Tim down to the exit. We'll wait for you there," she offered.

He nodded and headed toward the nurse's station.

"Annalisa! Look at that thing. Do you know how to do it?" Tim's boyish excitement seemed little hampered by the afternoon's adventure. He hurried toward the funnel-shaped contraption.

"Actually, I do." She fumbled in her purse and found a handful of coins. Pointing toward the center slot, she said, "Put one in there."

Tim's eyes grew large in wonder as the coin spiraled its way slowly around and around to the small hole in the bottom.

Just as he was dropping in the last coin, Annalisa spotted Cade coming down the hallway. The disturbed look on his face had her stepping toward him.

"Cade? Who was it?"

"It was Janet Melton from the Pulaski County Department

of Health and Human Services. She wants to see me tomorrow."

"Why?"

Cade hung back and glanced at where Tim was fascinated with the spiral machine. He lowered his voice. "She wants to discuss the possible need of removing Tim from my care."

fifteen

Annalisa heard Tim coming down the hallway long before she saw him.

He burst through the swinging kitchen door. "Annalisa!" He threw his arms around her waist as if he hadn't seen her just last night.

"Tim, you look like you slept well." She squeezed the boy tightly.

Aunt Gertie entered the room at a calmer pace. "He slept like a log. Not sure I'd have agreed to share a room with him last night, though, if y'all had told me how he snored."

Tim jerked away from Annalisa and stared at the elderly woman with wide eyes. Annalisa stifled a giggle when Aunt Gertie gave the boy a broad wink.

His endearing grin quickly reappeared. "You're teasing me."

"So I am."

"Where's Mr. Cade?"

Tim's question was a natural one, but Annalisa hadn't thought it through. She glanced at Aunt Gertie and silently pleaded with her to offer a plausible explanation.

The older woman placed her hand on Tim's head. "He had to run to Little Rock this morning, but he left me in charge of you. He said you'd help me in the garden."

George and Marta walked in the back door as Gertie was speaking, followed by Matthew and Juan.

"I didn't know Cade was going to Little Rock today," George said.

Annalisa nodded. Cade had told her to explain the situation to the Winemillers, but she'd wait until after breakfast when the children weren't around.

The subject quickly lost appeal as both George and Marta greeted Tim warmly. After they were satisfied he was okay, he ran to hug Matthew, who returned the embrace with a relieved smile. Tim started to throw his arms around Juan, but the teen stepped back and held up his hand instead. He grinned at Tim's enthusiastic high-five, though.

After George thanked God for the food, everyone but Annalisa and Aunt Gertie tore into the biscuits and eggs with abandon. Annalisa looked at the clock and caught Aunt Gertie's understanding gaze. It was time for Cade's appointment right now.

Dear God, whatever it takes. . .please don't let Cade lose Tim. She hesitated. *Unless it's your will for Tim's life, Lord. In Jesus' name, amen.*

"—and anyway, I didn't think a dumb old pillow would hurt you. And neither did Matthew." Juan's words were belligerent but his tone was apologetic. "You did start it, Tim."

"It wasn't cause y'all hit me with pillows, anyway, Juan. It was an asthma attack. I used to have them at home." Tim's words faded away as he obviously thought of unhappy times.

"You're right about one thing, Juan." George's stern voice was tempered with love. "You boys shouldn't have been playing with Marta's new pillows. She went to a lot of trouble making those."

She hand-stuffed them with feathers herself. George's words from an hour or so before Tim's first attack resounded in Annalisa's head.

"Were you pillow-fighting when you began having trouble breathing, Tim?" Annalisa asked the question casually.

His mouth full of eggs, he nodded.

George started talking about the horses. Annalisa laid her fork down and quietly excused herself from the table.

❧

"Good morning, Mr. McFadden. I'm sorry to have kept you waiting."

Waiting? She'd had him cooling his heels for an hour, after he'd risen with the chickens in order to be here at her appointed time.

He forced a polite nod. He couldn't afford to allow his irritation to show.

"As you know I asked you here because of the phone call I received from the Randolph County Emergency Room last night. When we approved your contract for the boys' ranch, I had serious doubts and now. . ."

Cade's cell phone rang. He froze. A quick glance at the caller ID told him it was the ranch. They wouldn't call right now unless it was an emergency.

"Can you excuse me for one minute? I have to take this." Cade offered a conciliatory smile and backed out of the room, clutching his phone. As soon as he was in the hallway, he answered, "Hello?"

"Cade, it's me. Guess what Tim and the boys were doing right before the asthma attack?"

"Annalisa, I'm in the middle of the meeting."

"I know! This is important."

"They were grooming the horses and feeding them hay. We've been over this."

"Yeah, well, Tim left out one little detail. What they were doing right before the attack was fighting with Marta's new pillows. Her feather-stuffed pillows."

"Feather pillows?" Cade knew he sounded boggled, but

this information was astonishing. Here was the element Dr. Johannsen had been looking for.

"And that's not all. Marta had just done her decorating the day before Tim's first attack at the ranch."

"Perfect, Annalisa. I'll call you later."

Cade walked back into the meeting with a much better attitude. "I have some news concerning Tim's asthma attack yesterday."

As he explained about the pillow fight, the stern-faced woman nodded. "I had asthma myself when I was young. I used to have an attack every time I spent the night with Aunt Betty. We finally figured out that while our pillows were foam, hers were stuffed with feathers. It made all the difference." With a stiff nod, she stood and extended her hand. "I'm sorry to have taken up your time. You may as well know I felt I had no choice but to take Tim out of your care. I still think that ranch of yours is a risky proposition, but it looks like this time you're off the hook."

Cade shook her hand and left the office quickly. When he stepped out into the bright sunshine, he decided to walk to Holt's office.

At the first street corner, there was a display of brochures for the upcoming State Fair. He picked up a flyer and thought of how excited the boys would be if he could take them. How wonderful to be going home to all three boys, including Tim. He'd been so afraid he was going to lose the child. . .first at the hospital, then this morning in that meeting. Was that how Annalisa had been feeling for seven years?

He yanked up his cell phone and quickly dialed. "Ronnie? Remember that case I mentioned to you?"

"You mean the one that was seven years old?"

"Yes, that would be it."

Cade held his breath. If Ronnie had found nothing, he would be under no obligation to Annalisa.

"You're always trying to stump me, Boss. But you'll have to try again."

"You found her?"

"Easy as pie. That little girl's still in the system."

"She's never been adopted?" Cade stopped walking and sank down on a corner bench.

"Not yet, but almost. Seems the father had been on again, off again in the girl's life, but he died a few months ago. The same family has had her from the time the state took her. They're about to make the adoption final."

Cade felt like his chest had been encased in concrete, making it impossible for him to breathe. Amy hadn't been adopted. Annalisa could probably claim her. But at what price? "You have the foster parents' info?"

"Sure thing. Hang on." As he heard the rustling papers through the phone line, Cade grimaced at the memory of Ronnie's cluttered desk. In spite of his employee's disorganization, the PI certainly knew his business. "Here it is."

Cade plucked a pen from his shirt pocket and turned the fair brochure over. He quickly jotted down the name and address in the margin.

He said good-bye, closed the little phone, and slipped it in his pocket. Lost in thought, he hardly noticed the gold-domed capitol building until he was almost past it. If Holt hadn't been expecting him, he'd have turned around and walked back to his vehicle.

When he reached his brother's office, Holt was on the phone. The senator waved his oldest brother into a chair and grinned. "Good to see you," he mouthed.

Cade nodded, but as Holt discussed Senate business with a

concerned constituent, Cade's mind drifted back to Annalisa and Amy. There was no easy answer.

"I said, you look like you've got the weight of the world on your shoulders."

Cade realized with a start that Holt had ended his phone conversation and was addressing him. "I'm sorry."

"You've got it bad, don't you?" Holt grinned.

"Yes, I probably do." Cade grimaced. "But that's not what's wrong."

"She doesn't feel the same way."

"I don't know." He realized that wasn't true. "Yes, I think she does. But there's more to it than that."

He gave Holt a condensed version of Annalisa's past and his current dilemma.

All traces of amusement vanished from Holt's face. "That's tough, Bro."

"Yeah." Cade brushed his hand across his face.

"Don't you think Annalisa would see that Amy is better off with the family she's known when it came down to it?"

"You've never seen such determination."

"Hmm. . . That's saying a lot coming from a McFadden."

"She makes us look like a bunch of quitters, Holt."

"What are you going to do?"

His brother's question lingered in the air. He didn't know the answer. "Pray."

"So will I."

"Thanks."

"Are you going to go see the foster parents?"

"Yes. I'm going to go this afternoon."

"Let me buy you lunch first?"

"You sure you've got time for a poor old cowboy like me?"

Holt glared at his brother. "Get real."

In spite of his bad mood, Cade smiled. He knew Holt despised it when his family insinuated he'd sold out to the glamorous world of politics. And, of course, they never could resist ribbing him about it.

Instead, he and Holt spent lunch talking and laughing about the antics of Cade's "boys" and Holt's colleagues. They studiously avoided the topic of Annalisa's sister. But all too soon, lunch was over.

Cade left Holt at the capitol steps and walked back to his car. He slid into the driver's seat and his troubled heart cried out for help to the only One who could give it.

Lord, please show me Your will in this. I'm confused and helpless. Guide my steps in Your way, please. In Jesus' name, amen.

sixteen

As Cade maneuvered the SUV through the well-kept streets of the sprawling, prosperous neighborhood, he could see Amy was at least provided for financially. One of Annalisa's fears could be laid to rest.

Even if he could banish all of her fears and prove that Amy was happy, would that be enough? He wished he could be sure.

He eased the car into the edge of the cul-de-sac and smiled. A brightly-colored Garage Sale sign adorned the mailbox next to the house number Ronnie had given him. When he realized it was Monday, his smile grew broader. A garage sale on a Monday was about as rare as a hard rain in the Sahara Desert, but right now it was equally as welcome. This would provide him the perfect cover to scout out Amy's adoptive home without raising suspicions.

He strolled down the driveway, focusing on blending in with the other customers. A slightly overweight woman in a neon green jogging suit was haggling with a young mother over a cradle.

"Thirty-five dollars? I only need it for those rare times that my daughter-in-law lets me keep my grandbaby. Since it's so close to closing time, would you take twenty?"

The two dickered back and forth, and Cade pretended to examine an old lamp. When voices came from the next door lawn, he turned and held the lamp up as if to see it better.

A giant red-headed man with a smile that seemed brighter

than the sun had his arm around the shoulders of a child. The little girl had the same bow-shaped mouth and big chocolate-colored eyes that Annalisa had.

Her brown hair was pulled up in a pert ponytail, but dark curls still cascaded almost to her waist. She bounced a basket-ball in one hand. Cade set the lamp down and stared as she tossed the ball through the basket.

"Nothing but air!" she crowed and high-fived the man.

"You're too good for me, little Missy." But he, too, spun around and shot the ball cleanly through the hoop.

"Aw, Red, I mean Dad. . ." Her already broad grin grew wider. ". . .you know I'm not as good as you are."

"You're not bad for a half-pint." He pointed toward her shirt and when she looked down, he gently tweaked her nose.

Her giggles resounded through the peaceful little cul-de-sac and even the green jogging suit grandma, cradle now in tow, cast a wistful look in that direction.

A petite woman of about thirty came out of the house with two glasses of something that appeared to be lemonade. "Amy? Red? Y'all thirsty?"

"Sure. . . ," the little girl paused, then continued, pride ringing in her voice, "Mom."

Cade frowned. According to what Ronnie had found out, the adoption wasn't actually final, but now that Amy's father was out of the picture permanently, the Montgomerys probably thought nothing could stop the adoption.

Time to rain on their parade, Cade thought grimly and crossed the small bit of grass from one driveway to the other.

"Mr. Montgomery?"

The tall man spun around, but his smile remained in place. "Yes? May I help you?"

"May I speak to you privately?"

Red Montgomery looked puzzled, but he nodded amicably and smiled at his wife. "Hon, why don't you and Amy go on in and figure out what you're going to wear to VBS? We need to leave in an hour and a half."

At the mention of Vacation Bible School, Cade mentally marked another of Annalisa's fears off the list. The child was being taught the Bible.

After his wife and the little girl were safely in the house, Red Montgomery turned to Cade. "What can I do for you?"

"I'm Cade McFadden." He extended his hand, and Red shook it without hesitation. Cade was already finding much to like about this easy-going man. In spite of his misgivings, he pulled a business card from his pocket and handed it to Red. "What I have to say is difficult. It's about Amy."

Red glanced at the card. He looked toward the house and frowned. "What about her?"

"Her sister is looking for her."

"Her sister?"

"She's twenty-four now. She was seventeen when social services took Amy away."

"And she's looking for Amy?" Red's voice cracked.

"Yes, she doesn't know yet that I've found her, but she wants to raise Amy herself."

Red's florid face went pale, and he collapsed onto a bench that looked purely decorative. It certainly didn't appear that it would support a man his size, but Cade was grateful it did.

"This can't. . . We can't. . ." Tears filled his eyes. Such raw emotion looked out of place on the big man's happy face, but his pain was as palpable as the hot July sun.

"Listen," Cade spoke gently, "maybe she would agree to a compromise. If we could settle this without going to court or anything, would you allow Annalisa to see Amy? To spend time with her?" He finished his appeal and held his breath.

Red put his face in his big hands and didn't move for a minute. When he looked up, he shook his head. "Mr. McFadden, you don't know what you're asking. Amy came to us as a baby. We never had children, and she was our first foster child." He bent Cade's business card into a triangle, concentrating on it, as if it were a most important task. "Of course we hoped to adopt her, planned to, actually, but every time we'd think we were about to sign papers, her father would show up and refuse to give up his rights." Red looked up at Cade in despair. "He never mentioned that Amy had a sister."

Cade squeezed his shoulder.

Red cleared his throat. "Anyway, last year, after he found out he had lung cancer, we invited him to stay with us. He started going to church, and I believe he truly repented of the hard life he'd lived. He became a Christian shortly before he died." Red flicked an invisible spot of dirt off the wrought iron arm of the bench, then looked back up at Cade. "But that doesn't change the fact that because of him, Amy's been a foster child instead of a Montgomery for the last seven years."

Cade winced at the man's statement. How wonderfully close this child was to a state of belonging. And not belonging to a stranger, but to the people who'd loved and cared for her since she was a year old.

"I understand."

"Do you?" Red shook his head again. "I'm not a hard man, Mr. McFadden, but Amy's sister hasn't seen her in seven years. I'd just as soon keep it that way."

Cade nodded. What would he tell Annalisa?

As if reading his mind, Red spoke. "Do you think you could live with yourself if you just didn't tell her you found

Amy? I can't believe I would even ask you, but I don't think my wife and I could bear to lose that little girl now. She's our daughter, in every way, except legally."

Cade nodded again. "I'll do what I can, Mr. Montgomery." He shook hands with Red and turned to go.

"God knows you're doing the right thing."

The man's words echoed in Cade's head as he drove back to the ranch. Did He really?

❧

Despite the good news about Tim, the day seemed to stretch out immeasurably with Cade absent. Would it be any easier when she was the one gone? Annalisa wondered as she cleaned up the supper dishes. Maybe she'd be so engrossed with finding Amy and winning custody that she wouldn't have time to miss Cade or the Circle-M. And maybe she'd grow another head and two more pairs of arms.

The swinging door opened, and Aunt Gertie came in. Looking around the sparkling kitchen, she shook her head. "Honey, you need to get out of here. It's beyond immaculate."

Annalisa sighed. "I know." She tossed the dishtowel on the counter. "I think I'll go out and check on the boys."

"That sounds like a plan. I think I'll settle in with a good book." Aunt Gertie lightly embraced her, and Annalisa returned the hug. She'd grown accustomed to the older woman's affectionate nature. Just one more thing she'd miss, she thought gloomily, and walked out toward the bunkhouse.

She could hear the voices inside, but the porch swing looked so inviting that she sank down into it. The sky was a swirl of colors, and the orange ball of the sun was sinking out of sight. A light breeze brushed her face. Laying her head back, she closed her eyes.

She must have dozed because the sound of a car engine

permeated her consciousness, and when she opened her eyes, the moon shone brightly in the night sky. The sight of Cade striding across the yard toward her made her sit up straight.

Before she could rise, he stepped up onto the porch and sat down beside her. "Hey."

"Hey." She turned her hand palm up and relaxed when he entwined his hand with hers.

"You have a good nap?"

"I guess. There's been so much stress. I didn't sleep well last night."

He rubbed his free hand down his face. "Me either. And today has been one of the longest days of my life."

Concern knotted in her stomach. He sounded awful. "Cade, what's wrong?"

"Nothing you can fix. I'm so thankful Tim gets to stay, aren't you?" His smile looked tired and a little forced.

"You know I'm thrilled." She was puzzled by his evasiveness, but hated to push him.

"You should be a private investigator. It didn't take you any time to put the puzzle pieces together and figure out Tim was allergic to feathers instead of hay."

"You hiring?"

"I need you here." His smoky eyes shimmered in the moonlight.

Annalisa opened her mouth to tell him she was quitting, but the words stuck in her throat. Something about his stance looked so vulnerable, and he'd admitted it had been a long day. Tenderness for this man she'd grown to love overwhelmed her. She'd tell him tomorrow. "I'm glad you made it home okay."

"It feels good to hear you say that—home."

"We'd better get to bed. I think the bunkhouse bunch has already turned in." She nodded toward the dark front window.

He stood and pulled her up, then held her hand as they walked to the big house. When they reached the back door, he tugged her to a stop.

He reached out and caressed her face, and by the light of the porch light, she looked up into the unfathomable depths of his eyes. A shiver coursed through her. He had the tortured look of a veteran who had seen things too horrible to mention. But when he lowered his mouth to hers, she forced the unpleasant thoughts from her mind and surrendered herself to the sweet purity of his kiss.

seventeen

Cade awakened with the memory of the back porch kiss still on his lips.

Judas. He'd kissed Annalisa last night, knowing beyond a doubt she'd despise him if she knew the truth. The kiss had been the ultimate betrayal.

He showered and dressed slowly. Since he'd come to the ranch, he'd been eager to meet each new day, but today was an exception. He didn't know how he would face her. It had been hard to hide his deception in the dark, but in the sunlight, it might prove impossible.

He'd questioned his motives all the way home last night. Had he truly agreed to stay silent because it was best for Amy? Or did he simply want to have Annalisa to himself, without going with her through the hassle and heartache of a court battle? Every time his resolve to keep the secret weakened, though, he remembered Amy, laughing and tossing the basketball with her "dad" or chatting happily with her "mom" about what to wear to VBS.

There was no guarantee that Annalisa wouldn't find Amy on her own. But—his stomach clenched at the thought—a week from now, after the adoption was final, it would be harder for her to do anything about it. The question now was whether Cade could live with that kind of responsibility for the rest of his life. Was he just a genius at bad choices? Or was God heaping more guilt on him to see how much he could take before he broke? The last thought gave him pause.

Could he turn this all over to God? He'd tried, hadn't he?

Suddenly unsure, he knelt beside the bed. The weight on his shoulders immediately lightened. He remained there talking to God for a long time, and when he rose, Cade knew he wasn't the one in control. There were no easy answers, but trusting God was the first step to a solution.

&

"Tim, turn the plates toward where the water comes out. Here, let me show you." Juan patiently took the plate from the younger boy's hand and rearranged it.

Annalisa beamed at the sight of the boys working so well together. The grin faded as she remembered how oddly Cade was acting today.

He'd been avoiding her. At first she'd thought it was her imagination, but when lunch was over, he'd hurried out without speaking, leaving Aunt Gertie and the Winemillers lingering over dessert. The day Cade McFadden turned down coconut cream pie was the day something was very wrong.

Tim pulled on her sleeve. "I gotta go to the bathroom."

She nodded, and he scurried out the door to the hall.

"He always has to go to the bathroom when it's his turn to help with the dishes." Juan grinned.

"Yeah, some people are like that. Tim's just starting early."

They worked in silence until Tim came bounding back in the swinging doors. "Look! Look what I found in Mr. Cade's room." He held out a brightly colored paper.

"Tim! What were you doing in Mr. Cade's room?" She took the paper.

The boy stared at her, innocence shining in his eyes. "I wasn't in his room. I just walked by on my way to the bathroom. This was on the table by the door." He pointed at it. "It says there's going to be a fair!"

Annalisa smiled and looked at the flyer. Pictures of carnival rides and animals pranced across the glossy white page. Maybe she'd still be here if the boys did get to go. She turned the paper over to check the dates.

The word Amy leaped out at her. Her knees buckled, and she sank onto the barstool.

"Annalisa?" Tim grabbed her arm, and Juan came over to stand beside her.

"Why don't you boys go tell Mr. George about the fair?"

"Okay!" Tim hurried out.

Juan lingered, concern evident in his dark eyes. "Are you alright?"

"Yeah, I'm fine. Go and keep an eye on Tim." The words slipped from her lips of their own accord, but thankfully the teen left.

Red and Vicky Montgomery. The names were scrawled below Amy's, followed by an address Annalisa recognized as being in an upscale Little Rock neighborhood.

Her heart felt like a concrete block in her chest and her arms and legs tingled. Cade had found Amy and kept the information from her. The man she'd fallen in love with had deceived her about the most important thing in her life. The room grew dark, and she bent forward placing her head between her knees. She couldn't faint now. She had to get her things and get out of here. Now.

ঝ

Cade wasn't surprised to discover his long walk after lunch had ended up at the barn. He'd always sought comfort in horses. That was one reason he'd worked so hard to help Annalisa learn to ride. It hadn't taken long for her to feel safe with Bubba and that was something she desperately needed—security.

As he approached the barn, he slipped into the game he often played with Duke. He'd slide stealthily up to the barn, and the horse would whinny as soon as he knew Cade was near. When Cade got to the barn door, instead of the horse's familiar nicker, he heard a human voice he didn't recognize.

"I almost did it again. If Tim hadn't been all right, I don't know what I would have done." The youthful speaker's throat was obviously clogged with tears, and his words were punctuated by loud sniffs. Cade peeked in the barn and spotted Matthew's head bowed close to Old Sweetie. "They'd have gotten rid of me, for sure. Nobody would want me around if they knew the truth."

Dear God, please give me the right words.

He took a hesitant step into the barn, and Duke whinnied loudly from his stall.

Matthew's head shot up and his green eyes, filled with tears, stared at Cade in dismay. Backing as close to Old Sweetie as he could, the boy cowered like a cornered animal as Cade approached.

"Hey, Matt. How's it going?"

Matthew turned his face to the horse's neck, and Cade saw his shoulders shaking slightly.

With another prayer, he closed the distance between them and slid his arm around the boy. "You didn't make Tim sick by hitting him with a pillow. He's allergic to feathers. Do you know what allergic means?"

Matthew nodded but didn't look up.

"We're actually kind of thankful you all had a pillow fight. Otherwise these attacks might have gone on and on, without us knowing what was causing them. And we might have lost Tim."

At Cade's last words, Matthew peeked out from behind his

arm. Cade nodded. "That's right. The state was going to make Tim live somewhere else because they thought he was allergic to the hay." He smiled gently. "It would be hard to have a ranch without hay, wouldn't it?"

The boy nodded.

"Were you in the accident with your parents?"

He nodded.

"Were you hurt?"

He shook his head.

"Want to talk about that night?"

He shook his head vigorously, his eyes wide.

"Because of something I did, a man died. I didn't do it on purpose, but that doesn't make it any better." As Cade said the words, moisture clouded his vision. He blinked and reached for Matthew's hand. The boy didn't resist. "It was awful."

Matthew nodded, but Cade could see the struggle in his face.

"It's weird that your parents were killed and you weren't hurt, isn't it?"

Matthew shook his head.

Cade held the small hand in his big one and waited. Other than a soft horse snort now and then, silence stretched over them like a warm blanket.

"She unbuckled to fix me a sandwich."

The words were barely a whisper in the quiet barn, and Cade had to lean forward to hear him.

"My dad and her were arguing. I was hungry, and he wouldn't pull over. She undid her seat belt and turned around on her knees to get to the cooler."

The silence stretched so long, Cade thought that was all he was going to say.

When he began to speak again, his voice was still quiet, but it trembled. "My dad said, 'Fine, if you're not wearing one,

I'm not either.' He popped his seat belt undone." Tears gushed down the boy's face. "I told 'em to forget it 'cause I wasn't hungry anymore, but they didn't pay any attention to me. My mom just kept slamming lunchmeat and bread around and griping at my dad." Matthew started sobbing, but it was as if once he'd started talking he couldn't stop. "All of the sudden, my dad said, 'Oh, no!' and slammed on the brakes. My mom fell sideways into him, and that's the last thing I remember."

He slid down the horse as if his legs wouldn't hold him.

Great, gulping sobs wracked his body, and he fell onto the straw. "Why didn't I unbuckle too?"

Cade couldn't keep back his own tears, and he collapsed beside him, gathering him into his arms. "Oh, Matt. It wasn't your fault."

The boy crawled into Cade's lap and keened, the high-pitched cry filling the barn. "Yes," he gasped, "it was."

"Your parents were adults. They knew better than to unbuckle. You didn't make them do it." He stroked the boy's hair, as his own tears mingled with Matthew's. "They were irritated with each other, and they used poor judgment, but it had nothing to do with you, Son."

Matthew buried his head in Cade's shoulder and shook his head.

"Matt, have you ever played a board game?"

He nodded.

"You know those little men you push around on the board?"

"Uh-huh."

"Your parents were playing a grown-up game right then. They were angry, and they were using you in their game. But, you weren't in control, Matthew." He grabbed the boy by the shoulders and forced Matthew to look in his eyes. "They were."

"They caused the accident?"

"No, they didn't cause it. It was an accident, a terrible thing that happened. But they chose not to be buckled in. You didn't choose it for them."

"Do you believe that?" He wiped his nose with the back of his free hand and regarded Cade with eyes that looked much older than their nine years.

Do I? Suddenly, it felt as if scales were falling from Cade's eyes. Annalisa's words about his own feelings of guilt came rushing back to him. Joey's father had been responsible for taking his own life. Cade didn't choose it for him. And he couldn't choose Amy's fate either. As soon as he and Matthew were done here, he was going to tell Annalisa the truth.

He met the boy's gaze unwaveringly. "Yes, Matthew, I do."

Matthew stared at him as if he wanted to believe.

"And even though they were upset with each other that minute, they both loved you very much. It would make them sad to know you were blaming yourself for the accident."

"You really don't think I made them die? You're not scared of me?"

Cade opened his mouth to speak, but instead pulled the boy to him again. They clung together for a few minutes, and there were more tears, but the tears this time were a catharsis for both of them. When they finally stood, Cade took a good look at Matthew.

He hadn't been transformed to a carefree boy, but the shadow that always lingered over his face wasn't there anymore. Cade knew Matthew would need counseling, but for right now, he was just thankful to hear his voice.

eighteen

Everything Matthew had been holding inside came pouring out like a sudden summer shower. He told Cade about Tim's asthma attack and how scared Matthew had been when he thought he'd caused it. For the first time, he put into words how exciting it was to catch a big fish. After they got Old Sweetie back in his stall, Cade gave Matthew a one-armed squeeze and kept his arm around the boy's shoulders as they walked together back to the bunkhouse.

George and Marta, as well as Aunt Gertie, seemed to realize too much attention would embarrass Matthew, so they tempered their excitement, but Cade saw the delight in their smiles. Once Cade was sure Matthew could handle Tim's curious questions and Juan's good-natured teasing, he slipped out to tell Annalisa the good news.

The house was eerily quiet, and Cade's heart sank. Surely she hadn't gone out without telling someone. "Annalisa!"

The countertop, usually scattered with preparations for the next meal, was clear, except for a folded white envelope with his name on it.

He opened it and read the scrawled writing in disbelief.

> *Cade, Tim was right. I did trust you. But I was wrong. Thanks for locating Amy for me, even if you weren't going to tell me. I've gone to get her. Please don't come after me.*

She signed it simply *A*.

154

She'd found the paper with Amy's name on it. A year ago, he wouldn't have been so careless, but since he'd been at the ranch, he'd let his guard down. He was sure a psychologist would claim he'd done it on purpose, hoping Annalisa would discover the secret he had been reluctantly keeping.

He ran down the hall to her bedroom. It was clean and empty. He tried to find something. . .anything. . .that indicated she might be coming back. But all evidence of her presence had been eradicated from the space.

He walked back to the kitchen and slid onto a barstool where just a few days ago he and Annalisa had talked about their feelings for each other.

God, why didn't You make me see sooner that I should have told her?

He rubbed his face with both hands, hoping to clear away the despair that coursed through his mind like a poison gas. He'd done this to himself. He had no one else to blame.

"Cade?" His aunt's voice broke in on his dismal thoughts. She stood in the doorway. "What's wrong?"

"Annalisa's gone."

"Gone?" Worry clouded her eyes. "For good?"

He nodded.

"But, I thought. . . The two of you. . ." Her voice faded off, but Cade knew exactly what Aunt Gertie had thought. He'd thought. . .hoped the same thing and, for awhile, Annalisa had shared his feelings.

He took a deep breath and started at the beginning. When he finished, his aunt was beside him, holding his hand. "Cade, you have to go after her."

"I can't." He ran his fingers through his hair. "I don't know how to explain it, but I know one thing. I have to give up control. . .even if I never see her again, which looks pretty likely at the moment."

"Oh, Cade. Is there anything I can do?"

"I'd like to be alone." He squeezed her hand and silently pleaded for her understanding. "Do you mind taking some supper stuff over to the bunkhouse for everybody? There should be some lunch meat in the refrigerator."

"I'd be glad to." She stood and hurried around the kitchen gathering food.

Soon, she was gone, and Cade was left alone again with his guilt.

He could ignore the last line in Annalisa's letter and go after her, but there was no point. She'd never trust him again. And he couldn't even blame her.

Dear God, please give me strength. I'm turning Annalisa over to You. I know I have no control over her life or even over my own. Take my future and make it whatever You would have it to be. . .

❧

Annalisa maneuvered her car down the gravel road. The scenery rushing by on either side reminded her of the day she and Cade had taken Tim to meet the ambulance.

Had Cade known then? While she was praying frantically he wouldn't lose the boy he'd grown to love so much, had he been sitting beside her, concealing the most important information in her life?

She trembled at the thought and banged her hand on the steering wheel. The car fishtailed, and she eased her foot off the accelerator. It was only another mile to the highway, then she'd be able to go faster. The more distance she could put between her and the deceitful man back at the Circle-M, the happier she'd be.

As the wheels turned, a chorus of self-recrimination sang in her mind. Why had she forgotten her promise? Hadn't her father's actions taught her not to trust a man? What had made her think Cade McFadden was the exception?

The long trip to Little Rock gave her plenty of time to come up with answers, but none were satisfactory. Whenever she'd allow the anger to diminish, reminiscences of good times at the ranch filled the quiet corners of her mind. By the time she'd reached the city limits, she had decided hostility was an easier travel companion than bittersweet memories.

She pulled off at the first exit and retrieved her Little Rock map from the sun visor. Within seconds, she'd located the street Amy lived on. Distance-wise, the house wasn't but a few miles from the area where Annalisa had been raised and Amy had been born. In every other way, the places were light years apart.

As she approached the cul-de-sac, all extra air seemed to leave her lungs, and her breath came in short, shallow bursts. Her heart thudded against her ribcage. What would Amy say?

Tears welled in her eyes, blurring the numbers on the mailbox. She killed the motor and stared at the beautiful house. After a few minutes, she gathered her courage and reached for the door handle.

Just as she had her hand around the cold metal, a tall, red-headed man came around from the backyard. She froze in her seat and watched as he walked up to a small tree in the front yard.

He stretched up to his tiptoes and peered among the branches. "Amy!"

At the sound of her sister's name, Annalisa squeezed the steering wheel and turned sideways in her seat to see more clearly out her open window.

When the child came running around the side of the house,

Annalisa gasped. She smiled, but tears rushed back to her eyes. Amy looked just like the pictures of her mother when she was small.

"Did the eggs hatch?" Annalisa soaked in the sound of her sister's voice after all these years.

Red Montgomery nodded and held out his hands. When Amy ran and jumped in his arms, he swung her up on his shoulders. She squealed with delight.

A shiver ran through Annalisa. That kind of happiness couldn't be faked.

"Mom!"

A petite brunette with gardening gloves on came around the house. "Hey, you two! What's going on?"

"Come see the baby birds," Amy called. The woman hurried over, climbed up on a big rock, and the little family stood together admiring the newborn birds.

Annalisa lifted her hair off her sweating neck and held it up on her head. She didn't want to start the motor and turn the air conditioner on, for fear she might miss hearing something Amy said. As she sat with one hand on her head and the other on the back of her neck, Red Montgomery's gaze met hers, and he held it for several seconds. From this distance, she couldn't see his exact expression, but she shivered again. He almost looked like he knew who she was.

He glanced back at the nest that was holding his family's attention. "We'd better go in and get ready for VBS," he said, lowering Amy to the ground. Holding hands, they walked together into the house.

United, Annalisa thought. *What will happen when I tell them? Will they splinter apart, or will they close ranks against me? Either way, I have to do it.*

She sat in her car for another hour, thankful for an evening breeze that blew gently through her open windows. She felt like a marathon runner who sat down a few inches from the finish line and refused to cross.

Please, God, give me the courage to do what I need to do.

The garage door opened, and a nice, mid-sized car eased out of the opening. Annalisa turned her face away as they left. She looked at her watch. If they were going to Vacation Bible School, they should be back in two hours.

Guilt stabbed her. While the Montgomerys were at church making sure her sister learned God's will for her life, Annalisa was going to sit here in front of their house and plot to take her away from them.

Annalisa rested the back of her head against the seat. The emotional turmoil of the day had drained her. She hadn't fully recovered from the loss of sleep with Tim's ordeal, and her brain finally succumbed to the exhaustion.

Car lights shining in her eyes awakened her, and she watched as the Montgomerys pulled back into the garage. The door shut behind them.

Shutting her out. Was this her lot in Amy's life? To always be on the outside looking in?

nineteen

She opened the car door, but her legs refused to move. The thought of bringing pain to Amy, especially now since she'd witnessed the child's joy, rooted her to her seat. It would be better to talk to the adults after Amy went to bed. Annalisa would wait a reasonable amount of time and then go up to the door and confront the couple. She quietly eased the car door shut again.

Within seconds, the front door of the house opened, and Red Montgomery stepped onto the porch. He walked slowly down the driveway.

Annalisa shuddered. He would surely stop at the mailbox and retrieve the day's mail then go back up to the house. He didn't. He walked past the ornate mailbox and continued into the cul-de-sac, not stopping until he was standing right beside her open window.

Bending down to meet her gaze, his eyes widened. She felt certain he knew who she was, but kindness radiated from his expression. "Are you okay?"

She stared at him for a few seconds, suddenly unsure. "Yes," she stammered. "I just needed a place to think things through."

He nodded. "I'm praying for you." His quiet voice rang with sincerity.

She wanted to speak, to tell him why she was there, to demand he let her have Amy, but she was unable to utter a word.

Red Montgomery turned and walked away.

ã

Cade raised his head and looked through bleary eyes at the kitchen clock. Three A.M. Turning the light out and going to bed would be giving up hope that Annalisa was coming back. He couldn't do it. He was praying that God would bring her back if it was His will, but Cade was also praying that God would give him the strength to accept it if it wasn't His will.

There was so much about her he loved. Her quirky sense of humor and quick wit kept him on his toes. He feared everyone would seem dull when held up against the memory of Annalisa. He remembered her appreciation of God's power the morning they'd shared the sunrise. In many ways, in spite of her hard upbringing, she was as innocent as a baby. When the boys or he needed her, she'd always given selflessly.

Why had he refused to trust her with Amy's future?

He put his face back down into his hands and groaned another wordless entreaty to his Father.

A key rattled in the door, and he raised his head. Like a little child on Christmas morning, he rubbed his eyes at the wonder he beheld. A very rumpled, tired-looking Annalisa stood in the doorway. Tears filled her eyes as she held her arms out to him. He jumped up and gathered her into an embrace, breathing in her flowery shampoo scent.

"Thank you, God," he whispered.

"Amen." Annalisa's voice trembled.

Cade scooped her up and carried her into the living room. He placed her on the couch and knelt in front of her. "Are you okay?"

She nodded.

"Before you say a word, I have to tell you how sorry I am. I only found out day before yesterday, and before I knew you were gone, I'd already decided to tell you."

She reached out and took his hand. "It's okay."

"No, it's not okay. I should have told you immediately. I'm so sorry." He gently pushed back an unkempt curl from her face and looked into her eyes.

She reached out her hand and cupped his cheek. "Do you remember King Solomon?"

Cade stared at her again. Had she been attacked? Was she sick. . .delirious with fever? "What?"

"King Solomon. In the Bible." The strength in her voice belied her odd words.

"Yes."

"I stopped my car in the cul-de-sac where Amy lives and watched. She was with Red Montgomery, and she was so happy. Her laughter bubbled through the neighborhood."

Cade remembered the look of envy on the jogging-suited grandma's face and nodded.

"The love between them was palpable. She called him 'Dad,' and in a few minutes she hollered for her 'mom.' When the woman came out, the love simply multiplied by three." Tears rolled down Annalisa's face. "By four, really. . ." She managed a tremulous smile. ". . .but they didn't know I was there."

Cade pulled her into another embrace, shame filling him again that he had ever doubted this woman. Even if she'd thought she was going to take Amy from her family, he should have known her better.

While he sat close beside her on the couch, she relayed the events of the night, including her startling encounter with Red. "I prayed for hours after he went in. The whole house got dark, except one light in the front part. Every once in awhile I'd catch the movement of a blind, and I knew that big man was checking to see if I was still out there. I just kept praying, begging God to give me the courage to just go up to the door and tell them I'd come for Amy. But I couldn't do it."

Cade started to speak, but Annalisa held up her hand. "I need to tell you the rest." She took a deep breath. "About midnight, I was still praying and suddenly the story of Solomon and the two women popped into my head. Remember when the two women both claimed the same baby and Solomon said he'd just cut the baby in two pieces and give half to both? The real mother readily gave the baby to the other woman in order to save the child's life, and Solomon could see from her love who the baby really belonged to."

Was she thinking that if she was willing to give Amy up then the child must really belong with her? Cade wondered.

"A peace that has evaded me for seven years washed over me tonight when I thought of that story. My little sister is so blessed. She has the Montgomerys who love her like that mother did her baby. And she has me. I'll love her and pray for her every day of my life, although she'll never know it."

She reached over and took Cade's hand and squeezed it. "I looked for her all these years to give her what she was missing and, if I'm honest, to fill an empty place inside of me. Tonight, I realized she isn't lacking anything. She has the love of a family and the love of God.

"At first I felt really sorry for myself. Then I thought of you and the whole bunch here at Circle-M, and I knew I had the same exact thing she did. Neither of us were missing anything."

Cade pulled her to standing and enfolded her in his arms. When she snuggled against him, he smiled. "Have I told you lately how proud I am of you?"

"Hmm. . ." Her teasing smile warmed the last chilled

corners of his heart. "That's not exactly what I was looking for from you, but I'll take it for starters."

They laughed, then he remembered there were things she still didn't know. "Before we go there, want me to fill in the blanks about Amy's life?"

"Please."

He told her all that Red Montgomery had told him. When he explained about her dad's complication of the adoption proceedings, she sank down on the couch.

"That old rascal. In a way, the Montgomerys have been waiting for Amy as long as I have, thanks to him."

Cade nodded and sat down beside her. "But 'that old rascal' did repent. Thanks to the Montgomerys, he became a Christian before he died."

"I can't believe it." She closed her eyes and leaned her head against Cade's shoulder. He watched tears of joy seep from under her eyelids.

They sat in silence for a few minutes, then Cade cleared his throat. "Annalisa, as far as what you were looking for from me. . .you probably already know. . .but I wanted to tell you again." He paused and glanced at her, hoping to read her reaction.

Her mouth was slightly open, and her eyes were still closed. When he leaned his ear toward her, her even breathing confirmed his suspicions. She'd fallen asleep in the middle of his declaration of love.

twenty

Annalisa rolled over and stretched in the sunshine that streamed across her bed. She opened her eyes and pushed herself to a sitting position. The little alarm clock beside her bed showed ten o'clock.

She jumped to her feet, then looked down. Why had she slept in her clothes? Memories of the day before pounded into her sleep-numbed mind like a herd of stampeding cattle.

The last thing she remembered was sitting beside Cade on the couch. She must have dozed off. Her sandals were on the floor by the bed, so apparently he'd carried her in and taken her shoes off.

She sat back down on the edge of the bed. A knock sounded on the door.

"Come in."

The door opened slowly, and Aunt Gertie, her hands laden with a tray, eased into the room. Bacon, eggs, biscuits, sausage, French toast, juice, and milk weighed the platter down. The older woman transferred her burden to the antique dresser and turned to Annalisa with a smile.

"Did you have to make breakfast? I'm sorry."

Aunt Gertie shook her head and grinned. "Cade insisted on fixing it himself. He took the boys on out to the barn, but I told him I'd listen for when you woke up and bring it to you." Tears filled her eyes, and she leaned forward to embrace Annalisa. "I'm so glad you're home."

"Me too." She returned the woman's hug.

"I'd better get out of here and let you eat in peace."

"You sure you don't want to share this food?" Annalisa arched an eyebrow at the tray. "I'd say there's more than enough."

Aunt Gertie shook her head. "Thanks, anyway, Hon. I've already had breakfast. I'm going to go listen to my radio program while I finish my coffee."

After the woman left, Annalisa fell back across the bed and lay there basking in the sunshine. She almost laughed as she remembered asking God to give her the courage to do what she needed to do. She'd meant so she'd be brave enough to fight for Amy, but he'd given her the courage to walk away, instead.

Now, in the bright light of day, she had lingering doubts. For seven years, she'd had one goal, and overnight, it was gone. The few minutes she'd heard Amy's voice and watched her laugh and play were infinitely precious, but abysmally short. Deep down, though, Annalisa knew she'd made the right choice.

Dear God, thank You so much for giving me courage and granting me a tiny bit of wisdom. And, Father? Thank You for bringing me home to Cade. In Jesus' name, amen.

Annalisa hurriedly ate and then showered. When she got to the kitchen all was quiet. She could hear Aunt Gertie's radio program playing in the den. The dishes had been cleaned up and the counter was clear, except for a white envelope with her name on it.

She tore into it with trembling hands. What was that cowboy up to now?

Meet me in our secret garden—C.

Anticipation raced through her. "I'm going outside," she

called to Aunt Gertie.

"Okay, Dear," the woman called back from the den.

Annalisa soaked in the familiar surroundings as she walked out to the rose garden. She slipped quietly around the barn, so she wouldn't run into anyone. The last thing she wanted was to be detained.

She pushed open the white gate and stared at the group assembled on the swing. Juan, Tim, and Matthew, sat side-by-side, broad grins on their faces. When she approached them, Juan cleared his throat. "Welcome," he said and nudged Tim, who giggled.

"Home," Tim said and nudged Matthew.

Annalisa realized with horror they expected Matthew to say something. What could she do to ease the awkwardness for him? Where was Cade?

The redheaded boy's grin never faltered, though, as Annalisa looked on in dismay. "Annalisa," he finished proudly.

"Matthew!" He stood and hugged her. She looked at Tim and Juan. "Thank you. . ." Tears sprang to her eyes. "Thank you all."

"We've got something to ask you." Tim jumped out of the swing and began to scamper around her excitedly.

"Hold on there, Buddy." Cade's deep voice came from behind Annalisa. "I'll take it from here."

The three boys each gave Cade a high-five on the way out of the gate.

Annalisa sat down in the swing. "Cade, why didn't you tell me Matthew was talking?"

"Hmm. . .when was I supposed to do that? Before or after you fell asleep last night?"

She felt heat creep up her face. "I'm sorry. My eyes wouldn't stay open. I hope I didn't miss anything important."

"Nah." He grinned and reached in his pocket. "Just this." When he got down on one knee in front of her, she put her hand over her mouth.

Tears began to pour down her cheeks. "Cade, before I met you I never cried, now I'm just a private waterworks facility." She laughed through her tears.

"Annalisa Davis, if you'll do me the honor of becoming my wife, I promise to try to keep your tears to a minimum in the future." He kissed her palm, and shivers ran up and down her spine. He turned her hand over and slid a diamond and emerald ring onto her finger. "Will you marry me?"

She opened her mouth, but he put his fingers against her lips. "Wait. Before you answer me, I have to tell you something. I'm going to try to adopt the boys. I've been talking to social services this morning, and they don't think there will be a problem. They're going to call me back. Even Juan's grandmother says she's too old to handle him. I think she'd be happy to have him just a couple of weeks in the summer."

She pushed his hand off her mouth. "Yes!" She tugged on his arm and pulled him up beside her. "You're offering me a lifetime with the man I love, plus what I've been dreaming of for years. . .a family. How could my answer be anything else?"

"You're a wise girl." He grinned. "And I am one blessed man. I love you."

"I love—"

His cell phone rang, and he frowned.

"You too. But, answer it," she urged. "It could be social services about the adoptions."

He grinned at her enthusiasm, but flipped the little phone open and sank down beside her in the swing.

"Hello. . . Yes, this is he. . . Yes, she is. Just a minute."

His eyebrows knitted together, and he wordlessly handed

the phone to Annalisa.

"You're scaring me," she whispered as she took the phone. "Hello?" She laid her head against Cade's chest.

"Hello. This is Red Montgomery, and I think we may have sort of met last night."

"Yes, that's right. . ." Her heart thudded. "Listen, I'm sorry for making you uncomfortable."

"You haven't made me uncomfortable. If anything has done that, it's my own conscience. Vicky and I have been praying about you ever since Cade came to visit the other day. When I saw you last night, I could see what anguish you were going through."

"Mr. Montgomery. . ." Annalisa tried to keep her voice from shaking. "I've decided not to pursue custody of Amy. Last night, I realized that wouldn't be best for her." Cade brushed her hair lightly with his hand, and his support bolstered her. "Thank you for your prayers." She started to flip the phone shut, but the man's voice stopped her.

"Hold on, there! I need to talk to you." Red sounded confident and sure. She motioned Cade to lean in so they both could hear. "If you don't object to us going ahead with the adoption, it should be final right away. However, Vicky and I were hoping you'd agree to be a part of our family too. . .even if it's in an unofficial capacity. We'd like you to be a true sister to Amy."

Annalisa nodded, but words wouldn't come. Tears clogged her throat, and she sent a silent plea to Cade. He took the phone from her and wrapped his arm around her. She noticed his own voice was husky with emotion when he spoke.

"Red." He paused, and she could hear his heartbeat against her ear. "Ah, I understand." He gently caressed her hair. "Annalisa is overwhelmed, but she'd be thrilled for a chance to get to know Amy. You may have to extend your family some more to include me, though. She's just agreed to become my wife."

Although she couldn't make out his words, Annalisa could hear the excitement in Red's tone.

"Thanks. We'll call you right away. Best wishes with the adoption."

When Cade finished the phone conversation, they sat for a few minutes, without moving, the only sound coming from Annalisa's little hiccoughing sobs. Cade held her until they subsided. "So much for my promise to keep your tears to a minimum."

Her heart filled to overflowing, she gazed up him. "Happy tears don't count."

He pulled her to her feet and enfolded her in his arms. "As long as you keep me updated on the rules, I should still be able to fulfill my promise then," he teased.

As Cade sealed his promise with a tender kiss, Annalisa knew her search for love had finally come to an end.

A Letter To Our Readers

Dear Reader:

In order that we might better contribute to your reading enjoyment, we would appreciate your taking a few minutes to respond to the following questions. We welcome your comments and read each form and letter we receive. When completed, please return to the following:

Fiction Editor
Heartsong Presents
PO Box 719
Uhrichsville, Ohio 44683

1. Did you enjoy reading *In Search of Love* by Christine Lynxwiler?
   ❑ Very much! I would like to see more books by this author!
   ❑ Moderately. I would have enjoyed it more if

   _____

   _____

   _____

2. Are you a member of **Heartsong Presents**? ❑ Yes ❑ No
   If no, where did you purchase this book? _____

   _____

3. How would you rate, on a scale from 1 (poor) to 5 (superior),
   the cover design? _____

4. On a scale from 1 (poor) to 10 (superior), please rate the
   following elements.

   ____ Heroine   ____ Plot
   ____ Hero   ____ Inspirational theme
   ____ Setting   ____ Secondary characters

6. How has this book inspired your life?_____
   _____
   _____

7. What settings would you like to see covered in future
   Heartsong Presents books? _____
   _____
   _____

8. What are some inspirational themes you would like to see
   treated in future books? _____
   _____
   _____

9. Would you be interested in reading other **Heartsong
   Presents** titles? ❑ Yes   ❑ No

10. Please check your age range:
     ❑ Under 18   ❑ 18-24
     ❑ 25-34   ❑ 35-45
     ❑ 46-55   ❑ Over 55

Name_____
Occupation _____
Address _____
City_____ State_____ Zip_____
E-mail_____

New York

Welcome to New York. . .a state of skyscrapers and mountain ranges—and home to four women who face challenges as formidable as those tall buildings and rugged peaks. Can they climb above the obstacles to find the heights of hope?

Enjoy four diverse stories from a diverse state.

Contemporary, paperback, 464 pages, 5 $^{3}/_{16}$" x 8"

Heartsong

CONTEMPORARY ROMANCE IS CHEAPER BY THE DOZEN!

Any 12 Heartsong Presents titles for only $30.00*

Buy any assortment of twelve *Heartsong Presents* titles and save 25% off of the already discounted price of $3.25 each!

*plus $2.00 shipping and handling per order and sales tax where applicable.

HEARTSONG PRESENTS TITLES AVAILABLE NOW:

(If ordering from this page, please remember to include it with the order form.)